Children of the Ocean God

by

Kiran H. Dellimore

ii

Printed in the United States of America

First Printing, 2024

ISBN 979-8-3717-99326

You spring, you say, from earth's foul sod;

We, offspring of the ocean god!

Your heaven no heaven could be, I swear,

Could white and red men mingle there!

No! Keep your heaven: in deadliest hate

I'd turn me from its very gate,

And hell's own darkest terrors dare

If I on entering found you there!

(Excerpted from Hiroona: An Historical Romance in Poetic Form by Reverend Canon Horatio Nelson Huggins.)

For the spirits of the mighty Garifuna ancestors watching over us,
may you find solace and eternal glory through these words.

CONTENTS

Chronology

1498	'Discovery' of St. Vincent by Cristopher Columbus
1500s	Spanish report a large African population living among the Caribs
1627	English lay claim to St. Vincent
1635	French forces, led by Pierre Belain d'Esnambuc seize St. Vincent
1653	Two French priests arrive in St. Vincent to teach Christianity
1654	Inter-island council of Caribs agreed to fight to expel the French and British from the West Indies
1660	Carib revolt against French rule
1660/Mar31	Peace treaty signed between France, Britain and the Caribs. Dominica and St. Vincent declared neutral
1700	Le Barre de l'Isle geographical line drawn by the Governor of Martinique to divide St. Vincent between the Garifuna (i.e., Black Caribs) in the East and the Yellow Caribs in the West
1718	Eruption of La Soufrière volcano in St. Vincent
1719	First European settlement of St. Vincent by the French at Barrouallie
1723	British attempt to reclaim and settle St. Vincent
1748	St. Vincent reaffirmed as a neutral island not under European sovereignty in the treaty of Aix-La Chappelle
1762	St. Vincent captured by English forces under General Robert Monckton
1763	St. Vincent ceded to the British by the Treaty of Paris after defeat of France in the Seven Years War
1769-73	First Carib War occurs
1773	Signing of Anglo-Carib Peace Treaty. It marks one of the first times that Britain is forced to sign an accord with a non-white, indigenous people
1779-83	French rule of St Vincent after France captures the island during American War of Independence

1780	British attempt to retake St. Vincent repelled by combined French and Garifuna force
1780/Oct11	Great Hurricane of San Calixto, also known as the Great Hurricane of the Antilles, occurs
1783	English rule of St. Vincent restored by the Treaty of Versailles
1789-99	French Revolution takes place
1794/Feb4	First French decree abolishing slavery in its colonies
1794/Apr1	Start of First Brigand War in St. Lucia
1794/Jun	Victor Hugues arrives in Guadeloupe from France
1794/Oct	British driven out of Guadeloupe by Victor Hugues and an army of 2000 freed slaves
1795	British breach their treaty with the Garifuna
1795/*Feb21*	A battalion of British troops is defeated by a group of rebels led by Victor Hugues in St. Lucia
1795/Mar2	Start of Fédon's Rebellion in Grenada, led by Julien Fédon
1795/Mar5	Word reaches St. Vincent of Fédon's Rebellion in Grenada
1795/Mar8	Second Carib War begins with burning of the estate of Madame La Croix and massacre of its inhabitants
1795/Mar12	Garifuna Chief Joseph Chatoyé makes a declaration at Chateaubelair to compel French settlers to join the Garifuna in the war against the British
1795/Mar14	Garifuna forces amass on the summit of Dorsetshire Hill overlooking Kingstown. Chief Duvallé takes down the British flag, replacing it with the French Tricolor
1795/Mar14	Chief Chatoyé is killed by Captain Alexander Leith in an alleged sword duel on the summit of Dorsetshire Hill
1795/Mar17	Originally planned date for the start of the Second Carib War (intended to coincide with the new moon)
1795/Apr22	Battle of Rabot in St. Lucia (part of the Guerre du Bois also known as the First Brigand War)
1795/May	Colihaut Uprising in Dominica begins

1795/Jun19   Guerre du Bois (First Brigand War) ends with the British defeated and fleeing from St. Lucia

1795/Nov7   Encke's comet observed

1796/May25   British retake St. Lucia from the French depriving the Garifuna of one of their primary sources of reinforcements and rearmament

1796/Jun3   Lieutenant General Sir Ralph Abercrombie arrives in St. Vincent

1796/Jun10   Garifuna surrender to the British - negotiation of terms is drawn out over the next nine months

1796/Jun19   End of Fédon's Rebellion in Grenada

1796/Jul   Garifuna who surrendered to the British are exiled to Baliceaux island off Bequia, where they spend nearly nine months

1797/Mar10   End of Second Carib War with the arrival of the last Garifuna on Baliceaux island

1797/Mar11   Deportation of the Garifuna, including 722 men, 806 women, and 720 children, by ship to Roatan Island, off the coast of Spanish Honduras (escorted by the H.M.S. Experiment)

1797/Apr12   Arrival of the deported Garifuna on Roatan Island

Map of Hiroona (St. Vincent)

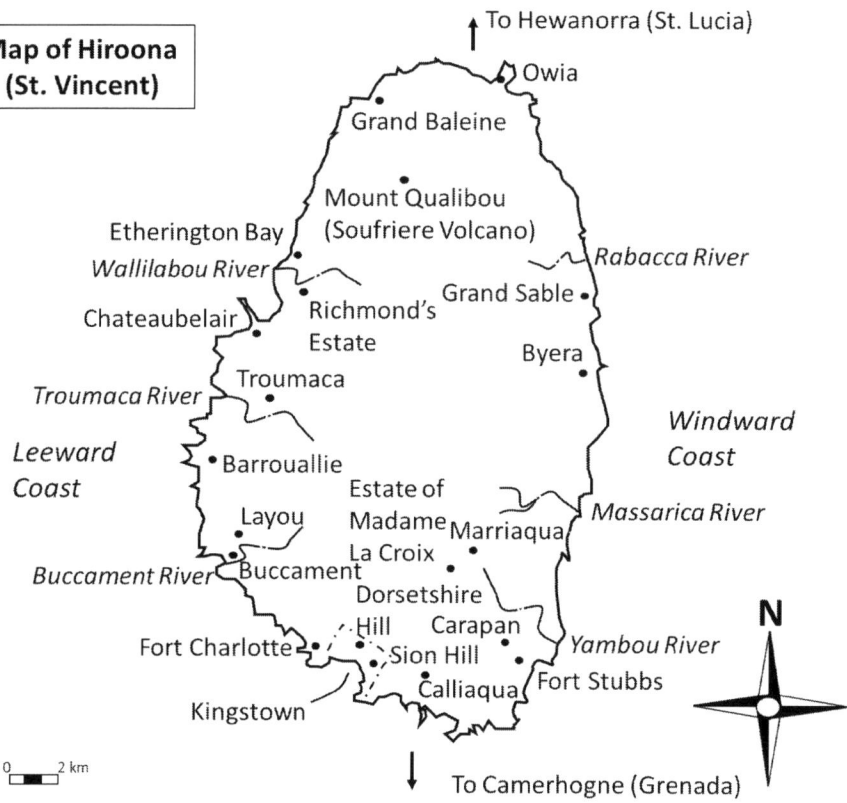

To Hewanorra (St. Lucia)

Owia

Grand Baleine

Mount Qualibou (Soufriere Volcano)

Etherington Bay

Wallilabou River

Rabacca River

Grand Sable

Chateaubelair

Richmond's Estate

Byera

Troumaca River

Troumaca

Leeward Coast

Windward Coast

Barrouallie

Estate of Madame

Marriaqua

Massarica River

Layou

La Croix

Buccament River

Buccament

Dorsetshire Hill

Carapan

Fort Charlotte

Sion Hill

Yambou River

Calliaqua

Fort Stubbs

Kingstown

0   2 km

N

To Camerhogne (Grenada)

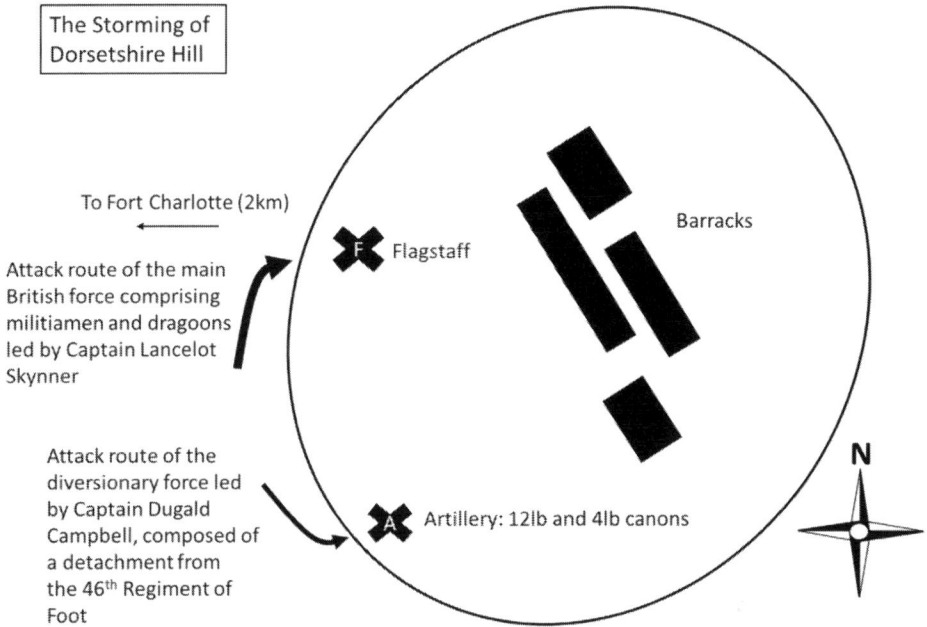

The Storming of Dorsetshire Hill

To Fort Charlotte (2km)

Attack route of the main British force comprising militiamen and dragoons led by Captain Lancelot Skynner

Flagstaff

Barracks

Attack route of the diversionary force led by Captain Dugald Campbell, composed of a detachment from the 46th Regiment of Foot

Artillery: 12lb and 4lb canons

N

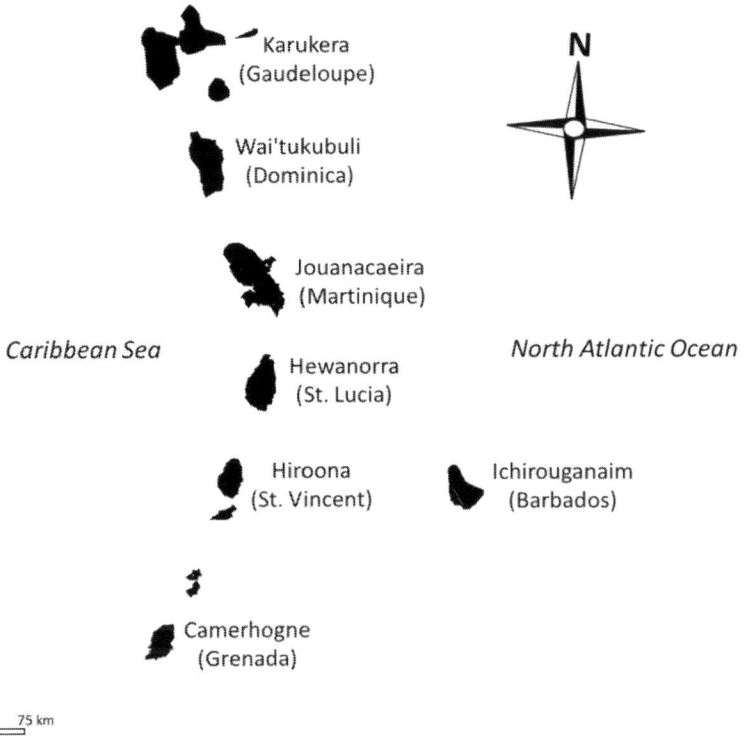

Indigenous map of the
Eastern Caribbean

Karukera
(Gaudeloupe)

Wai'tukubuli
(Dominica)

Jouanacaeira
(Martinique)

Caribbean Sea

North Atlantic Ocean

Hewanorra
(St. Lucia)

Hiroona
(St. Vincent)

Ichirouganaim
(Barbados)

Camerhogne
(Grenada)

0   25   50   75 km

Author's Introduction

The major events recounted in this novel are based on actual historical occurrences which took place in March 1795 prior to and during the first fortnight of the Second Carib War, on the Caribbean island of St. Vincent. Inspiration has also been drawn from the epic poem *Hiroona: An Historical Romance in Poetic Form* by Reverend Canon Horatio Nelson Huggins from which the title of this novel is derived. The main British and Garifuna (i.e., Black Carib) protagonists in the story are based on real-life historical figures. However, their personalities, dialogue and relationships with auxiliary characters are entirely fictitious. Any deviations from the historical record in the course of the narrative have been made through artistic license.

To enrich the story, I have intentionally included aspects of slavery, despite the fact that the Second Carib War was not directly linked to a slave insurrection nor had the aim of abolishing slavery. I have done this in order to highlight the awkward juxtaposition of free and enslaved Blacks that existed in St. Vincent prior to the war. It fed a simmering tension between the two groups, which fomented the powder keg situation on the island leading up to the conflict. Also, I wanted to make readers aware that slavery is inextricable from colonial Vincentian history.

While writing this novel I conducted extensive research into the culture, history, linguistics and traditions of the Garifuna people, in both the pre- and post-war period in St. Vincent. I did this out of deep honor and respect for the legacy of my paternal Garifuna ancestors, and to ensure that the story is authentic at the historical, sociocultural and anthropological levels. This was no easy task since the historical records are very limited, and do not capture the perspectives of the Garifuna about the war during the period of the conflict. Essentially my challenge as a writer has been to give voice to those who have been voiceless for over two centuries by piecing together disparate scraps of historical information. It has been without a doubt a labor of love.

The Second Carib War raged for over a year after the events described in this novel, and did not conclude until June 1796, with the defeat of the Garifuna. Tragically after surrendering to the British over four thousand Garifuna men, women and children were interned for nine months on Baliceaux island, which has an area of just 1.35 square kilometers and no natural sources of fresh water. There, disease, starvation and agony over their impending removal from their homeland ravaged the imprisoned Garifuna population. Subsequently, in March 1797 just two thousand two-hundred-and-forty-eight Garifuna survivors were deported to Roatan island, situated in present-day Honduras, seventeen hundred miles to the northwest of St. Vincent. I strongly encourage interested readers to seek additional resources to enrich their understanding and appreciation of this story. A useful place to start is the included Notes and Bibliography.

PART I – Perfidious Albion

Of the Greeks and the Romans let's imitate the courage!
Let us attack perfidious Albion in her waters!
May our annals opening with her destruction
Mark the days of victory!
May the world slowly be drawn towards us,
Feel from what burdens we will have delivered it,
And forgive us our glory.

(Augustin Louis, Marquis de Ximenes – excerpted from the poem L'Ere Republicaine, October 1793)

CH1

~~~

Warramou was struggling again with the restless spirits of the night. As he tried to fall asleep he could not get the ominous prophecy of the boyez out of his head.[1] *"The God Qualeva is angry at our people for adopting the false beliefs of the Europeans and forgetting our traditions.[2] He will punish us by bringing death and destruction to Hiroona unless much blood is spilled to appease Him."*[3] He kept replaying these words over and over in his mind, trying in vain to make sense of them. Surely this meant one thing. There would soon be war again in Hiroona. Yet he could not figure out how or why this fate should befall his idyllic homeland. The last war against the British was fought a generation ago, when he was a young boy, still living in his mother's hut. Only the boyez's mystical powers as a shaman, could have allowed him to read such obscure signs from the Gods.

In the faint bluish light of dawn Warramou gazed across at his second wife, Uwamá, lying beside him in the hammock with her soft, ample bosom pressed gently against his flank. He could feel the dull, rhythmic beating of her heart and the soothing warmth radiating from her body. Her breathing was deep and slow, indicating that she was peacefully asleep oblivious to his wakefulness. Not far away, just beyond Uwamá's head, he could make out his boutou leaning against the thatched wall of the hut. The intricate circular and rhombic patterns etched into the long, tapered mahogany slab appeared eerily like the tattoos on a warrior's arm in the early morning haze, belying the weapon's deadly intent.

As Warramou sized up the club in his mind's eye, feeling the weight of the boutou's violent power, his thoughts drifted back to the last time that he had wielded it in a moonlit raid on a village in the neighboring island of Wai'tukubuli.[4] A flood of emotion came over him as he remembered that fateful night. A night on which he wished he had heeded his grandfather, Pa Louen's, warnings in his dreams. It was the first time, his grandfather, who had recently died, had spoken to him in his sleep. He had warned him repeatedly not to let his younger brother, Lorain, join the raiding party. Yet he could not deny him the chance to join his inaugural battle as a Garifuna warrior. It was the culmination of Lorain's initiation into manhood. The fulfilment of his birthright since they were descended from a long line of great warriors, going back as far as Pa Louen's grandfather, who had defended Hiroona against the first European attempts to settle the island long ago.

In the thick fog of clubs, spears and musket fire, he had lost sight of Lorain's short sinewy frame. Later, he had found his brother's body crumpled on the ground outside a burning hut, bleeding uncontrollably from a gaping stab wound on his side. His nostrils flared as he vividly recalled the redolence of the

4

gunpowder and charred earth, mingled with the intoxicating mineral scent of fresh blood that hung in the air during Lorain's last moments. The bitter smell was so overpowering that he could still taste it on the back of his tongue. He would never forget how Lorain had howled in pain like a wounded manicou dying a slow death in his arms. Nor could he ever erase from his memory the look of horror and desperation in Lorain's eyes as he implored Warramou to save him. However, there was nothing Warramou could do to staunch the river of blood that was flowing from his brother. He had felt so weak and useless in that moment. It was a feeling that he never wanted to experience again.

These morbid thoughts were soon displaced by the gentle patter of footsteps rapidly approaching from the direction of Owia Bay. This struck Warramou as unusual. Normally the footsteps would be heading in the opposite direction at this time of day. The fishermen of the village usually left early in the morning from Owia Bay to catch flying fish. They were often so abundant there was hardly a need for a net to catch them as they would leap gracefully through the air until they haplessly landed in the fishermen's dugout canoes. They would return later in the morning with their canoes laden with fresh fish, ready to be fried up, then stewed in a creamy coconut broth and served with pounded ripe and green plantains. His mouth watered as he pictured the steaming bowl of savory hudut in front of him. Yet Warramou was certain of one thing. This was not a fishing expedition. The urgency and bearing of the footfalls meant that something out of the ordinary must have happened.

Warramou crept quietly out of the hammock, making sure not to wake Uwamá, before making his way towards the entrance of the doorless hut. As he emerged onto the dirt footpath in front of Uwamá's hut he could see his cousin, Eregu, running towards the hut of Irufugu, Chief Duvallé's youngest wife, a few hundred paces away. In his haste Eregu had not noticed Warramou's appearance. As he reached the front yard of Irufugu's hut he came to a halt and called out in a low voice, that Warramou could barely perceive, "*Chief Duvallé you must come at once. A French sloop has arrived bearing important news.*" Warramou could not make out the Chief's response, however, not long after, Duvallé's broad and burly silhouette appeared at the doorway of the hut.

From a distance, as the two men walked together, it was clear that Duvallé towered over Eregu, who was a full head shorter and more squat in stature. They were talking in soft tones as they headed towards Owia Bay where the French emissaries were awaiting them. As they approached his position, Warramou, called out a greeting to them, "*Buiti binafi. Good morning, brothers Duvallé and Eregu.*"

Despite being slightly startled by his presence, the men returned his greeting warmly.

"*Buiti binafi. Good morning, brother Warramou. You've risen early this morning!*"

6

"I heard footsteps approaching. So I came out to have a look. Besides I couldn't sleep anyway. What's going on brothers?" responded Warramou with an inquisitive look in his eyes.

"A French sloop has arrived in the night from Camerhogne bearing important news.[5] They have requested an audience with Chief Duvallé," blurted out Eregu, before Duvallé could offer an answer.

"Come join us Warramou. Let's see what the French want from us this time. I'm losing my patience with these endless congrès. These endless consultations. Every week they seek an audience with us. For naught!" huffed Duvallé, with a marked air of annoyance in his voice.

Soon, the three men were walking in Indian file, briskly down the steep, craggy path winding towards Owia Bay. There had been a thunderstorm in the night, so the morning air was damp and fresh. The soggy ground squished softly beneath their bare feet as they made their way.

While they walked, the men chatted about the latest happenings in the village. Eregu, who was always on top of the village gossip, brought up the recent feast hosted by Duvallé to celebrate the birth of his eighth child.

"I must commend you brother Duvallé, that was a sumptuous ouïcou, a sumptuous feast. The grilled iguana was heavenly and the tafia and guifiti were overflowing like the banks

of the Rabacca river in the rainy season. No one left the festivities walking straight."

Warramou and Duvallé both laughed heartily in agreement.

Eregu continued, *"And lest I forget all the beautiful goddesses from Grand Sable. Did you see the way Anigi looked at Warramou as she shook her hips?"* as he clumsily imitated Aingi's movements punctuated by several exaggerated pelvic thrusts. Eregu's gyrations were made all the more absurd by the awkward motion of his thick, stubby legs and the silly grin he wore on his face.

Warramou blushed. He indeed had an incurable weakness for beautiful women with luscious curves. Despite already having three wives, he still had a youthful penchant for chasing after love at every turn. At heart he was a romantic, who relished life's pleasures to the fullest.

Duvallé ribbed him further by mischievously adding, *"Uwamá wasn't playing the fool that night! After she saw you eyeing up Anigi, she put a stop to that like a hurricane sent by the God Obi.[6] Only divine intervention from the God Tamosi was able to save you from sleeping outside with the chickens that night Warramou."*[7]

"Ha Ha! So true. The gods have given Warramou a silver tongue, eh! He can talk his way out of anything." added Eregu with a devilish smirk, *"But the highlight of the evening was the clash*

between Chambo and Viteau. Yaw, that was the most brutal fight I've seen in years!"

"Yes! I tell you Chambo got his revenge good. His ichéiri are among the strongest in all of Hiroona![8] Some say that his good spirits are so powerful they have even protected him from evil by killing his enemies in their sleep." interjected Warramou excitedly, *"He waited till Viteau had finished a whole gourd of tafia before he made his move. Then he let his knife do the talking. Vicious!"*

"Yaw! Viteau didn't know what hit him!" added Duvallé letting out a loud peal of laughter. *"I heard that he's still recovering from his wounds. In fact, he hasn't been seen or heard from in over a week!"*

"That should teach him not to meddle with another man's woman. He's lucky he walked away with his manhood still attached! If it'd been up to me I wouldn't have let him off so easily," blustered Eregu, while stabbing the air ferociously, with his index finger imitating Chambo's deadly knife thrusts.

At that moment the pathway widened and split off into two opposing directions, heading to the north and to the south along the jagged coastline. It was there that the three men first caught sight of the French sloop through a break in the dense Manchineel foliage ringing the coast. She was anchored a stone's throw from the shore with her sails furled. The French Tricolor, flapping gently in the wind, was flying from her jackstaff, clearly visible, as were a half-dozen unmanned canons directed menacingly towards the shore. On the deck several men could be seen busily gathering barrels and sacks, preparing to load them onto a waiting skiff, tethered on the port side of the ship.

As always, Warramou was awed by the sheer power of European naval might. Their ships and guns dwarfed even the largest sixty-man pirogue that the Garifuna could muster.[9] Recalling the words of the boyez once more, he wondered whether the arrival of this French warship was another sign from Qualeva.

CH2

~~~

On the other side of the island Governor James Seton had also risen early on this morning. He crawled out of his large, mahogany four-poster bed, leaving behind his young, mulatto mistress, Josephine. She remained blissfully asleep, nestled amongst a mound of white linens and pillows. For a moment he cast an affectionate glance at her unclad form as the previous night's amorous embrace fleeted across his mind. However, this sensuous moment was short-lived due to other more pressing matters weighing heavily on the Governor's thoughts. He had in fact been awake for much of the night pondering these myriad problems, with no resolution in sight.

The chief concern bothering Governor Seton was that time was running out for him to make the Colony of St. Vincent prosperous like other British possessions in the West Indies. After almost eight years in office, there was growing impatience from London for him to prove his worth by lining the King's coffers with riches. He was keenly aware that the financial drain on the British Treasury for the defense and maintenance of the Colony was untenable. More was expected from a land of such vast untapped economic potential. However, the path forward towards prosperity for this 'restless' territory was obstructed by one problem that had stubbornly persisted since the first Europeans settlers arrived on the island.

The 'wild negroes' or Black Caribs, as they were sometimes called, were a thorn in the side of the Colony since time immemorial. They were blocking colonial territorial expansion through their possession of fertile lands in the northeastern, windward part of the island. This was a constant frustration for British and French settlers, especially near Calliaqua and Carapan,[1] who complained bitterly to the Governor that the fecund Black Carib lands, were hardly cultivated. If they were to be placed in the capable hands of European settlers, with a few thousand slaves, this land could easily be put to profitable use for cotton, sugar or indigo plantations. On several occasions in the past, attempts had been made to wrest the windward territory from them through various acts of chicanery, including a land survey and a futile attempt to build a road. However, they had all miserably failed in dislodging the stubborn savages, who remained firmly ensconced on the 'fine cream' part of the island, while giving themselves up to an idle, vagabond way of life.

Making matters even worse, was the scourge of runaway slaves who would regularly flee to the Black Carib territory. They would then be recaptured by the Black Caribs and illicitly sold back to the plantation owners for a tidy sum. It was expensive having free negroes in such close proximity to Black slaves. Ultimately this made the price of a slave in St. Vincent almost double that of

12

other colonies thereby hampering the Colony's fledgling economy. All the best efforts of the colonial administration to prohibit this duplicitous trade had failed disastrously.

Even more worrying was the Black Caribs' well-known alliance with the French, who were a persistent menace to British interests in the region. As Crown subjects, this intimate friendship with Britain's arch enemy bordered on treason. The Black Caribs could not be trusted and required continual surveillance in order to be kept in line. A Royal Navy frigate had in fact not long ago intercepted a corvette smuggling weapons and ammunition from the nearby French stronghold of Guadeloupe. It was also widely rumored that the Black Caribs were assisting the French revolutionaries in their support of the ongoing uprising in neighboring St. Lucia, which had started nearly a year ago.[2] British troops were heavily engaged there and had suffered a major setback, less than a fortnight earlier, with the rout of an entire batallion.[3]

All of these thoughts were drumming in Governor Seton's head as he knelt down at the foot of the bed to say his morning prayers. The Governor's piety was in fact not due to any particularly strong religious conviction. Rather it was driven in the first instance by his need for structure and routine in his life which had developed during his formative years at boarding school in England. Besides this force of habit, the Governor maintained his morning prayer ritual because of the mask of virtue it afforded him.

It permitted a certain moral latitude that kept his behavior above scrutiny. No one dared to question his actions, let alone hold him accountable for them. He was, at least in his humble estimation, regarded with great esteem not just in his household at the Governor's mansion, but indeed in all of the Colony and beyond its shores. Thus, praying each morning was a small price to pay for maintaining his sacrosanct veneer.

Once his devotions were finished, Governor Seton called his chamber slave, Koanda, to dress him for the coming day. Koanda, was a short, stocky, middle-aged but young-looking man of ebony complexion who was easily distinguished by a series of horizontal, tribal scars imprinted on his cheeks like whiskers. He was of keen intellect, yet often purposefully pretended to be slow-witted, especially in the Governor's presence, since he enjoyed the impunity it gave him to eavesdrop whenever matters of great importance were being discussed. Overall, Koanda possessed an agreeable disposition, however, at times he exhibited an almost imperceptible tinge of impudence directed towards the Governor which manifested in a slightly mocking tone of voice when addressing him or in an overly obsequious bow after performing a menial task at the Governor's behest. In spite of this, he was considered a dependable house slave, who took great pride in his status in the Governor's household and would never betray his master's confidence.

14

After grooming the Governor, Koanda served him *Hasty Pudding* and sweet *Bohea* tea,[4] on blue and white *Pearl White* porcelain,[5] recently imported from England. All the while, Koanda hardly uttered a word other than was necessary, since he sensed Governor Seton was in a taciturn mood this morning. Having worked for the past four years in the Governor's household, he had mastered the art of reading the Governor and knew precisely when he was best left alone with his thoughts.

As he swallowed his last swig of tea, the Governor summoned his aide-de-camp, Lieutenant Edmund George. Lieutenant George, was a sprightly young Englishman, of rather plain appearance and modest height, with a mop of curly brown hair. In fact, the only thing that stood out about him was his high-bottom posture, which gave him a mildly pompous appearance when he walked. He looked like a typical European struggling to cope with the sweltering heat and humidity of the tropics. His face, neck and limbs were a ruddy complexion from being frequently exposed to the blazing Caribbean sun, while the rest of his body was a sickly pale, vanilla tone. Despite being of officer's rank, Lieutenant George had a slightly unrefined air, betrayed by his overly common mannerisms and his incessant garrulousness, which frequently irked Governor Seton.

"Good morrow Gov'na, you're up early today! That was quite a thundastorm we 'ad last night sir!"

"Good day Lieutenant George. Yes, the weather lately has been absolutely dreadful. If it isn't stormy, then it's bloody hot and humid. Horribly unpleasant I tell you. Speaking of which, what engagements have I got today? I hope it's not going to be a horrid lot again."

"Let's see Gov'na. Hmmmph. Midmorn you've got your monthly council meeting wid da merchants and plantation ownas at Govament House, and at noon a visit to Fort Charlotte to meet wid Colonel Gordon to discuss da new fortification plans. Besides dat, da usual papa'work. A couple 'ah official documents to sign and letters to send out to da colonies. It's not too bad really."

"Let's set to work shall we? While I finish dressing, have Koanda send for the carriage, will you? Gramercy. Thank you, Lieutenant!"

Despite his early start, Governor Seton knew that he would likely not return home to the Governor's Mansion until nightfall. This meant he would sadly not see his son Robert, who was still fast asleep. Thankfully, he would be spared from having supper with his wife, Susan. He barely spoke to her these days anyway. Ever since she had been diagnosed with the *vapors* following several unexplained fainting spells, things had been awkward between them.[6] She spent most of her days shut away like a nun in her quarters in a remote corner of the Governor's Mansion. This had forced him to turn to the loving arms of Josephine. At least that is how he rationalized his infidelity to himself. Although,

16

truthfully he had been smitten with Josephine ever since he first set his eyes on her at a ball back in 1789.

It had taken him almost three years to connive how to steal her away from her ex-lover, a wealthy French planter from Chateaubelair. After contriving to have the Frenchman deported to Grenada on spurious grounds, he had conspired to have Josephine move into the Governor's mansion as a house slave while Susan was away on a voyage, visiting her sister in Barbados. For nearly a year he had carried on shamelessly with Josephine right under Susan's nose, until it became too much for Susan to bear. It was then that her mysterious illness manifested. After that, he despised Susan's presence, and would go to great lengths to avoid being around her. Every time he laid his eyes on Susan, the Governor would become disgusted with himself since it reminded him that he was a lecherous bedswerver. An adulterer, who swerves unfaithfully from his marriage vows.

In truth, the Governor had long been blind to Susan's feelings and her mounting dissatisfaction in their once loving marriage. After the death of their second child, Emma, in a candle fire he had never been intimate with her again. He blamed her for Emma's demise since she had been the last person to see her alive. Thereafter, no matter how much Susan implored him to take notice of her, he resisted and systematically shut her out of his life. That was when she had resorted to more dramatic means to capture his attention through her fainting spells. Yet these only

17

seemed to upset the Governor more and made him further estranged. It was at that point that he became more brazen about his shameful affair with her chamber slave. Infuriated and exasperated by his disregard for her feelings, Susan withdrew inwards and relegated herself to a nearly invisible existence on the fringes of the Governor's household. Her last thread of contact with the Governor, was their son Robert. Only in his presence did the Governor still grudgingly acknowledge her existence.

To complete his outfit, the Governor donned his blue formal jacket and bicorn hat, before heading out to perform his duties for the day. As he sauntered towards the horse-drawn carriage that would convey him to Government House, a Calvary officer approached on horseback bearing an important letter. From the grim look on his face, Governor Seton presumed that it was more terrible news from St Lucia. The British troops were taking a beating at the hands of the rebels there. Every passing day seemed to make withdrawal from the former French colony more likely. Surely things could not get any worse than they already were, he thought to himself, as he somberly broke the letter's official burgundy-colored wax seal.

CH3

~~~

When Chief Duvallé, Eregu and Warramou reached the seaside in Owia Bay, they spotted an empty skiff by the water's edge, accompanied on either side by small two-man dugout canoes, languidly bobbing up and down in the waves. It was low tide. The spirit of the sea was calm like a mother's soothing touch.

The French visitors were gathered at the far end of the beach, seated in a semicircle, together with two Garifuna watchmen, on makeshift stools made from stacked canvas sacks of salt and oaken tuns of wine that had recently been brought ashore. They all stood up in unison as the three men approached. When they were within a few paces, a tall, sturdily built, blonde-haired Frenchman, not long past his adolescence, addressed them speaking in French. Focusing his attention on Chief Duvallé he began in a formal manner:

"Bonjour most revered Chief Duvallé, I am Citoyen Touraille,[1] infantry commander of the French revolutionary forces in Guadeloupe."

"Bonjour Citoyen Touraille. Welcome to Hiroona our beloved homeland dear revolutionary brother. To what great honor do we owe the pleasure of your visit?" responded Duvallé in fluent French.

"*Our esteemed revolutionary leader Governor Victor Hugues has sent me to bring an urgent message to our Black Charaibe brothers in arms against the British.*"[2] Citoyen Touraille elongated the word 'Charaibe' as he spoke in his guttural, Marseillais drawl creating a peculiar timbre in the ears of Duvallé, Eregu and Warramou.

Hardly pausing a moment to catch his breath he continued, "*As you undoubtedly know, the revolution in St. Lucie is gathering momentum with each passing day. We have in fact not long ago decimated an entire British battalion.*[3] *Victory is near at hand. St. Lucie will be liberated soon! The British will be driven out forever!*"

This last boastful statement elicited raucous hoots and whistles from the four other Frenchmen present.

Citoyen Touraille continued passionately:

"*Most importantly, I bear news of the rebellion that has begun just three days ago in Grenada.*[4] *Our revolutionary brothers, led by the brave Citoyen Julien Fédon, have risen up in unison with the French settlers there against the British oppressors. It is only a matter of time before the forces of justice will prevail there too! Long live the revolution!*"

This drew even louder cheers and chants from the French revolutionaries, as they waved their scarves and hats in the air wildly, spontaneously breaking into song in French:[5]

"*Ah! It'll be fine, it'll be fine, it'll be fine*

The people on this day repeat over and over,
Ah! It'll be fine, it'll be fine, it'll be fine
In spite of the mutineers everything shall succeed.
Our enemies, confounded, stay petrified
And we shall sing Alleluia
Ah! It'll be fine, it'll be fine, it'll be fine
When Boileau spoke of the clergy
Like a prophet he predicted this.
By singing my little song
With pleasure, people shall say,
Ah! It'll be fine, it'll be fine, it'll be fine."

The news of the uprising in the neighboring island of Camerhogne had caught Chief Duvallé and his two companions by surprise. Being wary of the French, who were historically allies of convenience, they tried to disguise this fact, so that it might be of use to them diplomatically at a later stage. Nevertheless, the gleeful smiles painted on their faces betrayed the fact that they were very pleased to receive this news. Its implications were not lost on any of them. It meant that the British had their hands full with rebellions on the big islands immediately to the south and north of Hiroona. This made them more vulnerable to attack in Hiroona from the French. It was an opportunity the Garifuna had been waiting for since the last war they fought against Britain a generation prior.[6]

After the boisterous revolutionary singing subsided, Chief Duvallé pulled Citoyen Touraille to the side to continue their congrés, in private, while they strolled along the water's edge, away from the band of men.

Freed from the pressures of the group, the two men were able to speak more openly about the matter at hand.

Looking Citoyen Touraille in the eye, Chief Duvallé enquired directly, "*Let's not beat about the bush my dear Citoyen Touraille. Pray tell, what does His Excellency, Governor Hugues humbly seek to achieve through your visit to Hiroona?*"

"*My dear Chief Duvallé, I am entrusted to assure you that the French nation in combating despotism is allied to all free people: it desires nothing but liberty. It has always sustained the Charaibes against the repeated, vile attempts of the British to encroach on their lands. The time has come for the ancient friendship between the French people and the Charaibes to be renewed. We should exterminate our common enemy, the British.*"[7]

Citoyen Touraille paused briefly to allow his words to sink in before continuing further. His cheeks flushed red with excitement as he reached the climax of his message:

"*As you are no doubt well aware, the current posture of the British presents a most favorable opportunity to rid these Charaibe isles of the malevolent scourge of their occupation. The expedient extirpation of the British from the island of St. Vincent would further*

22

this effort and be to mutual advantage. Governor Hugues seeks therefore to induce the Black Charaibes to join the revolutionary fight against the British at this most prudent moment."

Duvallé calmly allowed Citoyen Touraille to finish what he was saying before offering a response.

"So the Governor is urging us to go to war with the British in Hiroona on France's behalf. Will our French revolutionary brothers also join us in the fight? Or will the Governor merely supply us with muskets and a little powder to do France's bidding?"

Without blinking an eye Citoyen Touraille flatly replied, *"We swear friendship and assistance in the name of the French nation to you and your comrades.*[7] *As fellow revolutionaries in the struggle for justice we'll fight shoulder-to-shoulder with the brave Black Charaibes until all the British in St Vincent are exterminated. Give us French only the means to second you. Our troops, canons, warships, and weapons, are humbly at your disposal."*

"This indeed makes the Governor's proposal more appealing. Yet as Governor Hugues surely knows, to engage in such a war we'll have to break our treaty with the British.[8] *This is a decision we shan't take lightly. As I can only account for myself, I must first consult with the other chiefs before offering His Excellency an answer. We'll send word once an appropriate course of action has been decided."*

The two men exchanged a firm handshake and then headed back in silence towards the group of men at the other end of the beach. By this time the northeasterly winds had started to pick up tossing the waves higher and higher against the rocky shore, as if the sea could sense the turbid thoughts brewing in Duvallé's head.

In the meantime, Warramou and Eregu had been left with the four Frenchmen and two Garifuna watchmen, who were merrily downing a demi-john of tafia. Each man took a long draught, before passing the bottle onto the next man in the half-circle. The French revolutionaries were already well lubricated with alcohol. They reeked of wine, tobacco and dank, unwashed human flesh. Yet despite their inebriation and awful stench their joviality and bonheur were infectious. Soon Warramou and Eregu were happily enjoying themselves as they would at any Carib ouïcou. All that was missing were women and a good fight.

Before long the drunken French revolutionaries were again crooning in a cheerful cacophony in French:[9]

> *"To arms, citizens,*
> *Form your battalions,*
> *March, march!*
> *Let an impure blood*
> *Water our furrows!*
>
> *Arise, children of the Fatherland,*

The day of glory has arrived!

Against us, tyranny's

Bloody standard is raised,

Bloody standard is raised,

Do you hear, in the countryside,

The roar of those ferocious soldiers?

They're coming right into your arms

To cut the throats of your sons, your women!"

Warramou and Eregu were snapped out of their revelry by the abrupt return of Duvallé and Citoyen Touraille. The deadly serious look in Chief Duvallé's eyes clearly signaled that he wished to depart without delay. There was no time for carousing, when urgent matters were at hand. The two men stood up instinctively and joined Duvallé's side, as he took leave of Citoyen Touraille.

Conferring in low tones as they made their way back to the village and were out of earshot of the French, Duvallé gave Eregu and Warramou precise commands:

"Brothers, the God Tamosi has finally answered our prayers and sacrifices. We must seize this precious gift from the gods with both hands. The time has come to rid Hiroona of the British. Warramou, make haste to Chief Chatoyé at Grand Sable.[10] Inform him of the events in Camerhogne and request his assistance in planning for war with the support of our French allies. Eregu, send

25

word to the other chiefs from Grand Sable down to the Byera River. At nightfall we shall convene a council of war on sacred Mount Qualibou.[11] *Time is of the essence brothers! May Tamosi guide your steps! Bungíu buma! Go with God!"*

Without hesitation Eregu and Warramou took off running to execute Duvallé's orders. Both men felt a surge of exhilaration in their chests from their patriotic mission. As they set out, the Sun's rays were just beginning to streak over the distant horizon. The blanket of darkness was rapidly dissipating into a colorful kaleidoscope of red, orange, yellow and blue hues, illuminating furrows of clouds traversing the pristine morning sky. Soon all of Hiroona would wake up to find out that the Garifuna were on the war path.

CH4

~~~

Governor Seton turned pale after reading the first few lines of the letter. He could hardly believe what his eyes were seeing. As he read further he stopped perceiving the words on the paper, succumbing instead to his imagination which had started racing wildly towards a terrifying apocalyptic scenario. Visions of the Governor's mansion burning uncontrollably while marauding bands of slaves, armed with machetes and knives, patrolled the streets of Kingstown killing, looting and raping indiscriminately, flooded his mind. Unconsciously, an explosive surge of anger overtook him, causing his brow to furrow, his jaw to clench and his lips to become pursed in an grotesque scowl.

The Governor's intense contemplation of the letter, was only broken when the Calvary officer, who was still standing nearby awaiting further instructions, cleared his throat abruptly. This snapped the Governor back to reality. Regaining his gubernatorial composure, he quickly affected a more agreeable demeanor, masking his burgeoning rage with a thin smile.

After gruffly dismissing the Calvary officer, Governor Seton carefully reread the letter. He wanted to be certain that he had fully grasped its contents. The letter had actually been sent from the Colony of Grenada and not St. Lucia as he had initially presumed.

St. Georges, Grenada, 4th March 1795

My dear Governor James Seton,

I trust this letter finds you in more favorable circumstances than I regretfully do myself the honor of reporting to your Lordship. Since yesterday I have been compelled to declare Martial Law on the island due to a rebellion of the Negroes that has erupted in Grenville, Marquis and Gouyave, in the parishes of St Andrew and St John.[1] The Insurgents, buttressed by the treacherous French, are desolating the Estates; many of which have been plundered and burnt to the ground. Several British planters and their families have also been monstrously murdered in cold blood. It is with deep sadness and regret that I must further inform you that our most beloved Governor, His Excellency, Ninian Home, has been captured and is being held hostage by the Insurgents near Belvidere.[2] I have directed the Ninth and Fifty-eighth Regiments of Foot,[3] together with the local Militia to utilize all necessary force to subdue the rebels, free our dear Governor and reestablish Law and Order in the Colony. Accordingly, I have issued warrants for the apprehension of one free mulatto, Mr. Julien Fédon, and his brother, Jean-Pierre Fédon, who are co-conspirators leading this treasonous rebellion.[4] We request all possible military assistance from the Colonies. In particular, supplies of gunpowder are urgently needed to replenish our dwindling stocks at the Armory.[5] Every moment of inactivity must surely increase the evil within.

Yours sincerely,
Acting Governor of the Colony of Grenada,
Kenneth Francis McKenzie, Esquire[6]

The gravity of the situation in Grenada slowly sank in. Most alarming was the report that Governor Home was being held captive by bloodthirsty rebels. That was in fact Governor Seton's worst nightmare. He could only imagine how terrifying it would be to find himself at the whim of vengeful slaves. Or worse still, at the mercy of the heathen, wild negro savages. He was loathe to ever let such a tragedy befall St. Vincent under his watch. Thankfully the slaves in his colony were less numerous than in Grenada and scattered throughout the island, making it harder for them to foment such a rebellion.

It further dawned on Governor Seton that the Colony was now effectively isolated, as rebellions were raging in the two nearest large islands, St. Lucia and Grenada, lying directly north and south of St. Vincent. This made the Colony more vulnerable to attack by the French from neighboring Guadeloupe, especially since British forces would be heavily engaged in quelling the two insurrections. It also did not fail to cross his mind that the 'enemy within,' the Black Caribs, might also avail themselves of this opportunity by initiating a war. It was therefore imperative for him to do his utmost to protect the Colony by circumventing a French or Black Carib attack. With this in mind, it was clear to the

Governor that it would be impossible to assist Grenada militarily without compromising the Colony's security. It would be too great a risk in the present precarious circumstances. All he could offer Governor McKenzie were his prayers and moral support.

After folding the letter away and carefully tucking it into the breast pocket of his formal jacket, Governor Seton climbed aboard his waiting carriage without saying a word to Lieutenant George. A slight nod of the Governor's head was the only signal the coachman received before setting off. The dour look on the Governor's face made it clear that he was in a foul mood, and was best left alone during the short ride to Government House. Yet to Lieutenant George's surprise, after a few moments of deathly silence the Governor looked him straight in the eyes and spoke in a grave tone.

"*Lieutenant, it has come to my attention that an insurrection, instigated by the vile French, has broken out some three days ago in the Colony of Grenada.*"

"*Gadbobs. Good heavens, Gov'na! First St. Lucia and now Grenada. What's next?*" blurted out Lieutenant George, as he nearly fell out of his seat in surprise.

"*Oh, for mercy's sake, I wish I knew Lieutenant. Those savages even had the audacity to take poor Governor Home hostage. What a calamity! This news doesn't bode well for the Colony. Heaven forbid the French 'll try to stir up a rebellion here!*

We must take action at once. Cancel my appointments for the rest of the day. I must see Colonel Gordon as soon as possible."

"Aye sir! I'll send word for the colonel to meet you posthaste to debrief you on the status of the regiment and the Militia," offered Lieutenant George, with a shallow nod of his head, in acknowledgement of the Governor's command.

"Oh, and one more thing Lieutenant. For the time being, please keep this news to yourself. We don't want to cause any undue panic in the Colony or for this information to fall into the wrong hands. Is that clear?"
The stern look on the Governor's face left no doubt that he expected this order to be strictly followed.

"Aye Gov'na. Clear as day! Hand upon my heart I shan't say a word to no one." Lieutenant George crossed himself as he said these words.

Not long after, the dull grey, wrought iron palisades of Government House came into view moments before the carriage pulled up abruptly in front of the patina gates near the corner of McIntosh and Cyrus Streets. The two men alighted in silence. They were greeted with a stiff salute from the two on-duty sentries, dressed in their red-and-white ceremonial uniforms, mindlessly pacing back and forth between the two opposing guard posts, shouldering their muskets with bayonets fixed. As the pair walked briskly into the main building, Kingstown was just beginning to come to life. They could hear the not so distant sounds of the

31

hawkers arguing loudly while setting up their fruit, vegetable, fish and meat stalls in the market, as well as the shopkeepers yelling at their slaves sweeping their storefronts with cocoyea brooms in preparation for the first patrons of the day.[7] The smell of freshly baked bread and meat pies wafted lazily through the morning air mingling with the bilgy stench emanating from the sewers, lining the streets. It was the start of another miserably hot and humid day in Kingstown, impervious to the violent events occurring not far away in Grenada and St. Lucia.

The calm would not last much longer, that much was certain to Governor Seton as he sat down at his sturdy, waxed-honey-colored mahogany, kneehole desk to begin drafting an emergency proclamation. After completing this task, he wasted no time in writing a dispatch to Lieutenant General John Vaughn, the British military commander in neighboring Martinique. In the letter the Governor appealed for ammunition, arms and a detachment of troops from the Forty-sixth Regiment of Foot stationed there. He desperately hoped that they would arrive in time to avert a disaster in St. Vincent.

CH5

~~~

The sun was already high in the morning sky when Warramou reached Grand Sable. His brow was drenched in perspiration and his breathing was heavy from his arduous trek across the jagged, hilly terrain in the stifling tropical heat and humidity. When he arrived, the village was already bustling with activity. The women were busy preparing the first meal of the day, coconut bread and cassava porridge, while their children wrestled and played avidly at their feet. Several men were returning from having a bath in a nearby stream, while others were lounging around the carbet on stools playing reed pipe flutes.[1] The men's cotton hammocks were already neatly folded away against the stout mahogany posts supporting the carbet's thatched roof, made from dried palm fronds and cachibou leaves. Two young boys, not long removed from their mothers' huts,[2] could be seen busily sweeping the sandy floor of the large, oblong structure, which served as the center of daily life for males in the village.

Warramou searched for Chief Chatoyé at each of his five wives' huts, but did not succeed in finding him. His first wife, Reuma, however, offered a clue to his whereabouts.

"Buiti binafi. Good morning, brother Warramou. I'm afraid Joseph has left early this morning for Grand Baleine to check on the cotton and indigo harvest."[3]

"Buiti binafi. Good morning, mother. Do you know when he'll return? I come bearing an important message from Chief Duvallé."

"He usually comes home to eat before the hottest part of the day," replied Reuma nonchalantly. She dipped her finger into the simmering pot of cassava porridge to check the taste. Not satisfied, she added a few pinches of sugar which she gently stirred into the steaming gruel.

"I really must speak with Chief Chatoyé urgently," insisted Warramou, sensing that Reuma had assumed it was a social visit.

"It shouldn't be too long now my son. Why don't you wait here for him? I've just cooked some delicious cassava porridge and baked some fresh coconut bread. Why don't you have some?"

Given the urgency of his mission Warramou was reluctant to wait around and strongly considered heading immediately onto Grand Baleine, which was on the leeward coast of the island and would take him at least until mid-morning to reach. However, his fatigue and ravenous hunger soon prevailed, so he decided to avail himself of Reuma's hospitality. Her cooking was renowned in all of Hiroona, so it was hardly an inconvenience on his part.

"Seremein. Thank you, mother. I'll wait for Chief Chatoyé as you suggest. Some coconut bread and porridge would be delightful. I'm starving."

34

Reuma smiled warmly at Warramou in response and quickly fixed him a large bowl of steaming cassava porridge with two plump rolls of freshly baked coconut bread. He devoured everything like a man who had not eaten in a week. Afterwards, he washed it all down with a gourd full of refreshing spring water.

Having momentarily satisfied his primal needs Warramou turned his attention to his other motivation for coming to Grand Sable. He secretly wanted to see Ranné, Chatoyé's eldest daughter from Reuma, with whom he was madly in love. She was hands-down the most beautiful woman in all of Hiroona. Everything about Ranné was stunning; from her velvety dark, cocoa-colored skin, to her silky, long, wavy black hair flowing down her back. Although Ranné was keenly aware of her beauty's effect on men she did not flaunt it immodestly like some other Garifuna women. She always maintained a slight distance from men. Some might even go as far to say that Ranné was standoffish and cold to the less fair sex. Yet despite this impediment she possessed a distinctly lithe air, which had enchanted Warramou from the moment he had first laid eyes on her, when he was an adolescent.

However, Ranné was much more than a pretty face. She had from a very young age demonstrated that she was an atypical Garifuna female. She had grown up playing rough and tumble with the boys of the village, most of whom she could effortlessly outrun and outwit. Early on, she had discovered that she despised the mundane household chores that were the traditional domain of

35

women. Nevertheless, out of devotion to her mother, whom she adored, she forced herself to cook, clean and tend to crops. Unlike most Garifuna women, Ranné did not aspire to marry a great warrior and bear him male children who in turn would grow up to be fierce warriors. Although she admired her father for what he had accomplished as a paramount chief, she knew that she did not want her mother's life of servitude. Nor did she wish to be known as just Chief Chatoyé's daughter. She dreamed of carving out a niche in the world based on the merits of her own creative pursuits. Ranné was in fact fond of making clay pots, often in the shape of heads with wide eyes and large ears for handles, which were used to keep water cool and for preparing seasoned meat and fish. She would elaborately decorate them with intricate geometric designs using red, yellow and orange dye from crushed annatto seeds. This artistic outlet was her passion, to which she dedicated her every spare moment.

Warramou had courted Ranné relentlessly over the past two rainy seasons but she had repeatedly rebuffed his advances. She had made it clear that she had no interest in becoming his fourth wife. In fact, challenging Garifuna custom, she had even declared that she wanted a man all to herself as she did not relish the idea of sharing a man with other women. Yet, her father was fond of Warramou, and encouraged Ranné to give him a chance.

The last time Warramou had visited Grand Sable, he had again proposed to Ranné, and she had for the first time relented by saying that she would think about it and let him know her answer in due course. That was three full moons ago. So Warramou was eager to meet Ranné again to find out if she had made up her mind. Reuma, being keenly aware of all that had transpired between them, glanced knowingly at Warramou with a mischievous look in her eyes.

"*Why don't you go see Ranné while you wait on Joseph? I'm sure she'll be pleased to see you. She left not long ago to plant some pineapple trees in the orchard by the big Buffalo tree.*"[4]

Without hesitation, Warramou scampered out of Reuma's hut to search for Ranné. When he caught sight of her, his heart skipped a beat. Words failed to come to his mouth as he basked in the radiance of her immaculate beauty.

After a few moments, Ranné, sensing she was not alone, looked up from the hole she was intently digging and addressed Warramou:

"*Buiti binafi. Good morning, brother Warramou. Have you been there long?*"

"*Buiti binafi. Good morning, sister Ranné! It's been too long since I last laid my eyes on you!*"

"*What brings you here to bother me today? What have I done to Qualeva to deserve this? I'm sure you have more important manly things to do than watch a simple woman do her work.*" These last words Ranné spoke in a playful, mocking tone.

Ranné was about to lay into Warramou cheekily, as she often did, but she held her tongue mercifully after observing the vulnerable, adoring look in his eyes. Secretly, she loved the passionate way he always looked at her. It was not like other men, who stared at her lustfully like an object to be possessed for their selfish desires. Warramou always had a way of making her feel self-conscious. His intense gaze at that moment, reminded her of this, making her fall silent.

"I'm here on an urgent mission to see your father. Chief Duvallé sent me."

"What's happening now? Are the British planters encroaching again on our land? I hope this won't lead to another fight with them. Isn't that all you men know how to do? Fight and kill each other!"

"We shall see princess. Qualeva's will must be done!"

Warramou paused for a moment, before changing the subject, adopting a more serious tone, *"So, Ranné do you have an answer for me or must I continue to suffer?"*

"Not yet Warramou! I'm still asking Tamosi for His divine guidance. I'll let you know my decision soon, I promise."

"I'll hold you to that princess. May Tamosi grant you the wisdom you seek."

With a devilish grin, Warramou added, *"It has done my heart much good to see you again. You're looking well!"*

Ranné blushed and looked away from Warramou shyly.

"Seremein. Thank you, Warramou. Go now! I must finish my work here before helping Mama with the cooking so that it'll be ready when Papa returns."

Warramou quietly withdrew to the carbet to await Chatoyé's return. To pass the time he replayed in his head his previous encounters with Ranné, desperately trying to interpret her feelings towards him. He hoped she would soon give him the answer he desired.

Not long after, Chief Chatoyé showed up. He was a sturdy, well-proportioned man with broad shoulders, of above-average height, who had a handsome mix of Carib and African features. His high cheekbones, broad flat nose, copper colored skin, and long raven-black locks, piled in a tuft on the top of his head and wrapped in a pale, red cotton turban, accorded him a quintessential Garifuna look. This was completed by his palm-fiber loin cloth, waist-mounted dagger and large, golden earrings in both ears. However, most characteristic of all, was Chief Chatoyé's demeanor. He possessed a dignified, calm manner that commanded respect from friend and foe alike.

Chief Chatoyé was in fact the most decorated Garifuna warrior of all time. He had achieved legendary status due to his brilliant leadership during the First Carib War, a generation prior. It had been a brutal war of attrition, with the British invading their communities and wantonly burning their cassava fields, costing many lives due to starvation. Yet they had resisted successfully,

39

through his clever guerilla tactics. The most famous of all, celebrated in the Wanaragua dance at many an ouïcou,[5] was his deadly strategy of warriors disguising themselves in women's clothing. This caught the British soldiers off guard when they raided their villages, as they did not expect to face male resistance. The conflict eventually ended in a stalemate, with the signing of a peace accord, placing the Garifuna on equal footing with Great Britain, the most powerful nation in the world. This treaty had affirmed Garifuna freedom by establishing their right to the land in the north of Hiroona along the windward coast. It was for this reason that Chief Chatoyé was widely revered by his fellow Garifuna, as well as highly regarded by the French and British.

He seemed unsurprised to see Warramou.

"*Buiti amidi. Good afternoon, brother Warramou. I heard from Reuma you're looking for me.*"

"*Buiti amidi. Good afternoon, father. How's the harvest?*"

"*We had a decent yield of cotton and indigo this time! Our efforts in the fields are finally paying off.*"

Looking into Warramou's eyes Chief Chatoyé added with a knowing smile, "*But I can see in your face that you're not here to talk about my plantation, are you? What brings you to see me? Has Ranné finally made up her mind? Or is she still playing coy and stalling for time? I keep telling her to accept your proposal but she doesn't listen to her father.*"

As he uttered these last words Chief Chatoyé gazed at Warramou warmly. There was something about Warramou that reminded him of his younger self, although he could not put his finger on it precisely. Part of it had to do with Warramou's tendency to never back down when faced with a challenge. It was almost impossible to dissuade Warramou, once he set his mind to something – including his desire to marry Ranné, which was reminiscent of Chief Chatoyé's own relentless pursuit of her mother, Reuma. Equally redolent were his impressive skills as a warrior in combat, in particular his keen grasp of military strategy. In his mind it was clear that Warramou had the right temperament to one day become a great Garifuna chief. It would not take long for him to realize his potential as a leader of their tribe.

"I saw Ranné earlier. Unfortunately, she hasn't made up her mind yet. In fact, I'm not here today to speak to you about Ranné."

"I read immediately on your face that your visit had another purpose," offered Chief Chatoyé perceptively.

Looking him squarely in the eyes, as if he was attempting to read Warramou's thoughts, he added, *"So, what urgent matter brings you here today brother?"*

"A French sloop arrived last night at Owia Bay. They've brought news of a rebellion against the British in Camerhogne. The French are agitating for us to wage war against the British here in Hiroona. Chief Duvallé requests you to join the council of war to be convened this evening on sacred Mount Qualibou."

41

Chief Chatoyé nodded his head in acknowledgement of all that he had heard. It was clear by his measured response that nothing was lost on him.

"This may indeed be a most opportune moment for us to attack our British foes. I'll ask the boyez to perform a ceremony this evening to be certain that such a war is the will of the Gods."

His stomach let out a low rumble, reminding him of his ravenous hunger, before he continued, *"I'm famished. Come, let's eat Warramou. Reuma and Ranné caught some crabs yesterday. I heard they're making your favorite dish; tumallen and crab with fresh ereba.*[6] *Afterwards let's visit brother Duvallé to make a plan on how to deal with the French. They're friends of convenience and can never be fully trusted. May Tamosi guide our judgement!"*

Warramou rubbed his belly with delight as he followed Chief Chatoyé to Reuma's hut. He could already taste the delicious stew, made with green crab meat, extracted from just under the shell, cassava and peppery, citrusy tumallen sauce, on the tip of his tongue. It was always better to discuss important matters on a full stomach.

CH6

~~~

Alexander crept out of bed and felt around the earthen floor of the dimly lit shack until he found his trousers. As he fumbled to pull them on, the persistent throbbing in his head reminded him that as usual he had drunk one pint too many the previous night. Even in his half-drunken stupor it was obvious how the night had ended. The stifling smell of sweat, grog and cheap pleasure lingering in the air said it all. Alexander grabbed his shirt, and boots and quietly headed out without saying a word to the slumbering negress that had quenched his carnal thirst.

The door creaked audibly as Alexander pushed it open. He instantly froze in his tracks, since he was not keen to wake his lover. She let out a low moan as she rolled over in bed. He waited for a few moments until her breathing returned to a slow and steady pace before resuming his egress. He grabbed the handle firmly and gently tried nudging the door open again. But once again it creaked loudly.

"*Blast!*" he swore under his breath.

It was too late. He was sure he had woken her up.

"*Mmhhhhh. Alex. Da's yo? Weh yo a go luv? Comb go back bed!*"

He responded to her with silence.

"*Yo betta nah mek me mash yo op in here Alex oyee. Me na mek fool anah!*"

He ignored her, yet still did not take a step further.

"*Yo betta na leave wid me moni! Ehhh heh is chubble yo fo wan so?*"

Alexander reluctantly reached into his pants pocket and fished a shilling out of his brown leather pouch. He then flung the coin impetuously in the direction of the negress while attempting to placate her by saying, "*That's all I've got Rosie! I promise I'll give you the rest next time love.*"

The coin ricocheted off the wall and after rolling around on the ground in circles settled near the foot of the bed. *Eish!* Rosie let out an ear-piercing shriek as she scrambled out of bed frantically trying to locate the money in the murk.

"*Mudawuk! How yo ah go an so? Ga 'way yo brute!*"

Alexander smirked to himself, then turned around and strode out the shack without saying another word. The door loudly slammed shut after him.

Roselind's lean-to shack was situated behind the back wall of the Anglican church, within crawling distance of his favorite tavern. This invariably made it Alexander's sleepover spot on his frequent binges of dissipation. As he tramped off, Alexander instinctively fingered the coins in his purse to find out how much money he had left after the previous night's carousing. He was disappointed to discover a paltry three shillings and a six-pence.

Barely enough to cover his expenses for the next two weeks, but it would have to do.

"*Blast! The Devil's been dancing in my pocket again,*"[1] he cursed to himself under his breath.

Alexander made a left onto North River Road, before taking a second left onto Grenville Street, one of the main arteries of Kingstown, which led towards his home. By now the sun was nearing its zenith in the late morning sky, and beating down mercilessly through an almost cloudless blue sky. He was already concocting an excuse to tell Mr. Farquharson as to why he had not shown up for work that day. He knew he had shirked his duties again. It hardly mattered anyway, he figured. His clients were already very wealthy Scottish plantation owners on the island and paid him, in his estimation, a mere pittance for the services he rendered as an attorney.[2] Although it was a position of some importance in colonial society, which he had worked hard to attain after starting out as a lowly bookkeeper,[3] he was still not content. He would never make a fortune working for this stingy lot of planters who lived in the lap of luxury off the backs of slaves and the starvation wages paid to hardworking men like him.

As Alexander neared the Bedford Street intersection he heard a strange commotion coming from the market square nearby. When he got closer he caught sight of a large crowd of men who were yelling and arguing vociferously.

"*I say my good man, do you know what's all this commotion about?*" he enquired of a short, middle-aged looking Englishman, with salt and pepper hair, hovering on the periphery of the crowd. From the appearance of his dingy, shabby looking satin waistcoat and soiled, worn through barathea wool breeches it was clear that he was not of high social standing. He looked like a bookkeeper who supervised gangs of slaves on a plantation in the sugar cane fields from dawn until midnight. Or perhaps he worked in a factory superintending the boiling of sugar, as Alexander had once done when he first came to the West Indies.

"*'Tis da Militia milord. Da Gov'na's just called 'em to arms, made a proclimation he did. Da bloody French and dem wild negroes up nort' mights be attacking us any day now. We gots to be prepared yuh know.*"

"*Gadbobs! Good heavens! Is that so? A call to arms. An attack by the French and the wild negroes?*"

"*'fraid so milord. Dere's a resurrection in Grenada and Saint Lucia yuh know. Dem fiends in Grenada have ev'n taken dear 'ol Gov'na Home hostage they have. Our lads have 'er hands right full. We could be next! I'm heading home to get me pistols. Firs' patrol starts dis evening it does.*"

Alexander, was surprised by the news, yet at the same time secretly thrilled by this new prospect. He was eager for some action to spice up his dull life in the tropics. He had in fact recently signed up to the Militia, by dint of his close association with well-

46

respected Scottish planters, Major William Lumsden and Mr. Macduff Fyfe.[4] In his capacity as an attorney, managing several profitable sugar estates for both men, he had finagled a plum commission for himself as a captain in the Militia. However, he had seen it merely as a means to raise his status in colonial society and had not anticipated getting called up to service anytime soon.

Excited by this unexpected turn of events Alexander headed home to sleep off the rest of his hangover, before reporting for Militia duty later in the day at Fort Charlotte. As he wended his way through the crowded streets of Kingstown, oblivious to the raucous commotion all around him, his thoughts drifted to the past. His life's trajectory had been tarnished by the tragic loss of his parent's wealth, in a family feud two generations prior, back in Aberdeenshire, Scotland.[5] He hoped that the impending action with the Militia would present an opportunity to regain his family's former prestige and more importantly offer a pathway for him to attain fame and fortune. That was what had brought him to the Ceded Isles in the first place back in 1771.[6] Alexander had long harbored a burning desire for grander social status. He had a feeling in his gut that on this occasion the stars were aligning in his favor. It would only be a matter of time before he would be elevated to his rightful place among the wealthy, landed nobleman owning hundreds of slaves.

Alexander was not alone in his surprise about the impending conflict. The news of the insurrection in Grenada had in fact spread like wildfire through the town. All around, people were scurrying to gather last minute supplies. Some were even trying desperately to book passage by ship to Barbados, a nearby British stronghold, fearing that St. Vincent would be next island to face strife. Yet in spite of this frenzy, several British gentlemen still took the time that afternoon to enjoy a maroon dinner with a number of Black Carib chiefs on a hillside overlooking Kingstown.[7] Unusually, more Black Carib men and women had come to town that day to sell their woven baskets and provisions in the market. Yet there was no sign of anything untoward. It was the lull before the inevitable storm.

CH7

~~~

The sound of beating drums could be heard long before Chief Chatoyé, Chief Duvallé and Warramou reached the summit of Mount Qualibou. As they drew closer and closer, the percussion of the drums became more deafening, until the three men could feel it reverberating in their chests as they emerged into a clearing illuminated by a ring of torches. There they found ten chiefs seated on the ground in a circle surrounding a large, flat, granite altar. On the edge of the clearing, lurking halfway in the shadows stood the boyez. He was easily distinguished by his long grey hair and thick, silvery beard, which was atypical for Garifuna men, and by the assortment of animal skins, shark teeth and mysterious coral talismans that draped his gaunt frame. In his left hand he was grasping a small, wriggling agouti by the neck while holding a dagger,[1] with a sharp, curved blade, in his right hand. All the while, he was chanting mysteriously into the wind while gyrating and contorting his body in various animated poses.

The arrival of Chiefs Chatoyé and Duvallé signaled the beginning of the ouïcou. A feast of iguana and manicou on the spit along with roasted cassava was served by several women while the chiefs drank gourds of red wine, cassava beer and tafia to their hearts' content.[2] As the men became more inebriated they began to dance wildly and sing boisterously about their proud Garifuna ancestry and their love for their homeland, *Yurumein*.[3]

> *"We are the mighty Garinagu!*
> *Across the vast Carib Sea*
> *We came from the river Orinugu[4]*
> *Sailing in destiny's canoe*
> *To Yurumein our beloved homeland*
> *Her beauty is beyond compare!*
>
> *We are the mighty Garinagu!*
> *Proud children of the Ocean God*
> *He guides and protects us always*
> *Through trial and tribulation*
> *We keep Yurumein forever in our hearts*
> *For she is the land of the blessed!*
>
> *We have no fear, not even death!*
> *We have no fear, not even death!*
> *There are no cowards here!*
> *We are the mighty Garinagu!"*

Emotions continued to rise further as each chief, in turn, aired their grievances against the British. Particular venom was reserved for the plantation owners who were encroaching on their, lands near Calliaqua and Carapan. Following tradition, the host of the ouïcou,[5] Chief Joyette, brandished a boucaned arm of a slain enemy from a previous war while haranguing the other men. He reminded them of past injustices they had suffered at the hands of their enemies, Garifuna and European alike. Subsequently he invoked them to seek revenge by settling their scores once and for all.

Shortly thereafter, the proceedings reached a fever pitch when Chiefs Tourouya and Kaierouane were persuaded by Chief Joyette to fight each other in hand-to-hand combat to settle an old score about a woman. The two men began grappling each other before drawing their daggers from their loincloths and making violent slashing movements in the air, while gnashing their teeth. Chief Tourouya drew first blood by gashing Chief Kaierouane's chest just below his right collar bone, which elicited raucous cheers from the onlookers. Like a true fearless Garifuna warrior, Chief Kaierouane's face was expressionless; showing no signs of pain despite the steady flow of blood gushing from his wound. Moments later he returned the favor by deftly slashing Chief Tourouya across the ribs with a lightning quick left-to-right cut. The two men continued to brawl for several minutes, until they were both doubled over, drenched in blood and sweat, gasping for breath.

At that point, Chief Chatoyé called the war council to order by blowing a lambis three times.

"My dear brothers it is no secret why we're gathered here this evening. The time has come for us to discuss the matter at

51

hand. We must consult the gods to see if it is their divine will that we break the treaty with the British." Chief Chatoyé spoke these words in a grave tone conveying his unshakable faith in the traditional shamanistic practices of his people.

Looking at the boyez, who was standing over the granite altar holding the now lifeless agouti, Chief Chatoyé nodded signaling that it was his turn speak.

"*O great chiefs, I have made the necessary sacrifices to the ancestors and Gods. No clouds appear across Hiroona's future nor have I received any sign of a phantom-bird in my ear. Qualeva sleeps and will not rise again until our enemies are vanquished! The omens for war are all good!*"

Chief Chatoyé smiled in approval that all signs portended favorably for war against the British. He then withdrew his dagger from his loincloth and placed the sharp edge of its curved blade against his left breast. Without batting an eyelid, he pressed it firmly into his skin until he drew blood, all the while showing no signs of pain. After the first drops of dark red fluid oozed out onto the blade he raised the knife into the air and declared:

"*On the blood of my fathers' fathers that runs through my veins I declare war on our British enemies. Who here among you dares to join me in this blood oath?*"

Each of the remaining eleven chiefs, one after the other, drew their daggers and performed the same ritual as Chief Chatoyé, before swearing unanimously to join the war.

52

Following Garifuna custom, the start of the war would coincide with the new moon, which would occur in ten days' time. This would give sufficient time for smuggling and stockpiling of weapons and ammunition from *Karukera*,[6] as well as careful coordination of their attack with their French allies. With the war council's decision confirmed, Chief Chatoyé sent word to Citoyen Touraille and his revolutionary compatriots to join them.

By the time the French revolutionaries arrived, the ouïcou had kicked into even higher gear. Several women, the wives of the chiefs, were dancing passionately – shuffling their feet with one hand on their head and the other on their hip – amid lively singing and flute playing.[7] The French were greeted warmly, with loud cheers and overflowing gourds of red wine, cassava beer and tafia.

Upon learning that the Garifuna had decided to wage war against the British, Citoyen Touraille stood up ecstatically and addressed the gathering in French, with revolutionary zeal:

"Bravo! Bravo! I assure you the whole of France stands behind the Charaibes. Together we shall defeat the British. Let us fall on these despots, extirpate them from this land, and restore yourselves, your wives and children to the inheritance of your fathers. Their spirits will lead on your ranks from the grave, inspire you with fury, and help you to be avenged. Together we shall prevail! Long live the revolution!"

This elicited a din of cheers, howls and whistles from all present. After the noise abated, looking into the kindling eyes of the Garifuna, Citoyen Touraille continued persuasively:

"We assist you from motives of the philanthropy and zeal for the happiness of all nations. The long and sacred friendship between our peoples is unbreakable. We shall stand by your side till the last Redcoat falls!"

He then very deliberately unfastened the sheathed steel rapier that had been hanging loosely around his waist, grasped it with both hands and lifted it up, while bowing deferentially before Chief Chatoyé saying, *"Behold, I present you, the most fearsome Chief of the Black Charaibes, with a gift from Governor Hugues. From this moment forth you are accorded the rank and privileges of General in the French Revolutionary Army."*

Chief Chatoyé nodded solemnly in acceptance of the honor.

As if suddenly overtaken by a maniacal spirit, Citoyen Touraille then leapt impetuously onto the stone altar, which offered a commanding view of the northern part of the island. While pointing towards the settlement of Vieux Fort on the neighboring island of St. Lucia, merely eight leagues away,[8] he boldly addressed Chief Chatoyé:

"O Great Chief look well and pray tell what do you see?"

54

Chief Chatoyé leapt up to join Citoyen Touraille on the altar and cast his gaze as instructed, while making a telescope with both hands.

"*I see a fleet of ships along the coast over yonder. If my eyes don't deceive me, I count at least nine. And from the distant hills I discern flashing lights.*"

With a proud, gleeful gesture Citoyen Touraille crowed:

"*Those are ships of war, redirected from Guadeloupe. Deliverance comes at last! They swoop on the British like birds of prey. Those flashes of light you see are the glean of bayonets from French troops manning the hills. The British have nowhere to hide. This too shall be their fate in St. Vincent. Let us attack Perfidious Albion in her waters!*"[9]

These words were hardly spoken before they were drowned out by a pandemonium of wild, drunken cheers from both French and Garifuna alike. With the support of the French affirmed, war in Hiroona was now assured. Nothing could stay destiny's fateful hand.

CH8

~~~

Meanwhile in Kingstown, the streets were unusually quiet. Governor Seton had imposed a curfew from dusk till dawn. He was taking no chances with his safety nor that of the Colony. Out of an abundance of caution, he had ordered several emergency defenses to be hastily erected at strategic points around the periphery of the city and instructed the Militia to begin night patrols. Fearing for his own life he also made plans to evacuate the Governor's Mansion and take up temporary residence in Fort Charlotte. Although it crossed his mind that this move would bring with it some drawbacks, as his mistress and wife would now be in closer quarters, it was nevertheless the best option to avoid the miserable fate that had befallen Governor Ninian Home in Grenada.

After an anxious yet uneventful night had passed, the residents of Kingstown woke up the next morning to a flurry of wild rumors. Many merchants were claiming that a French attack was imminent. Reports had reached the city that a French sloop had been spotted in the north of the island with several heavily armed French invaders already landed. Some even speculated that it would only be a matter of hours before they arrived in Kingstown to ransack it. Other stories claimed that an armada of French ships of war was on its way from Guadeloupe to seize the colony. They urged the Governor to send for military assistance from Martinique and Barbados without delay.

Amid the panic and frantic preparations Governor Seton found himself besieged by visitors, each of them concerned with their own selfish interests. Several planters wanted assurances of compensation from the Crown for the expected damages and losses from the coming war. Others, enterprising merchants, seeing an opportunity for profit, were trying to sell their stocks of provisions and clothing, at inflated prices, to the Governor in order to outfit the Militia. Still others, representatives of 'concerned' colonists, were urging the Governor to raise a regiment of armed slaves. Conveniently, the Crown, should pay them at a lucrative rate for the mercenary services of their slaves.

The Governor felt like a carcass being feasted on by a volt of ravenous vultures. It was only money and property that was on the minds of the planters and merchants. None of them seemed to care one bit about the impending danger to the Colony and worse still the looming tragic loss of human life that would surely occur. Disgusted by this moil, Governor Seton decided to stop taking visitors in the mid-afternoon.

"*Lieutenant George!*" he barked hoarsely.

"*Aye, gov'na!*"

"*I'm tired of this endless procession of opportunists and profiteers. They all seem intent on shamelessly fleecing the Crown*

coffers! Please see to it that the rest of my afternoon is cleared."
The Governor's voice was unmistakably edged with irritation as he spoke these words.

"Aye, gov'na. I'll get to it straight away!"
Before turning to head out, Lieutenant George added somewhat sheepishly:

"Gov'na. There's actually a man, one Mr. William Greig,[1] just come to see you about da wild negroes and such. Shall I send 'im away sir?"

After a brief moment of reflection, the Governor replied, *"Umm, no Lieutenant! Please send him in. Make this my last visitor for the day."*

"Certainly sir. I'll send for 'im directly," offered the lieutenant deferentially.

Despite feeling drained by the drudgery of his present duties, the Governor's interest was piqued by the mention of the wild negroes. They had been rather quiet of late and he was anxious to hear news about what they might be up to in light of the recent news from Grenada.

Mr. Greig was a prominent planter, who had been growing sugar cane in the Colony, since the island of St. Vincent was ceded to Britain back in 1783. He was an average-looking middle-aged Scotsman, of medium height, with a wrinkled forehead and long sandy brown hair, which was tied neatly at the back with a black ribbon. He was dressed fairly modestly, in plain off-white

58

breeches and stockings, with a matching short coat and waistcoat of checkered blue, green and red Tartan, and black leather riding boots. The most interesting feature of Mr. Greig was his bushy, walrus moustache, with its thick whiskers dangling over his mouth, which quivered every time he spoke. This gave him an oddly distinguished look, that stood out beyond his otherwise plain features.

Mr. Greig charged into the Governor's office like a man being chased by the devil. His brow was sweaty and he reeked of horse hair and dried blood. Without taking a seat, he addressed the Governor, while mopping his brow excessively with a bloodied cotton handkerchief and panting heavily:

"*Good day Governor Seton. Cahuh-cahuh-cahuh! Please forgive me for this intrusion, your Excellency. Cahuh-cahuh-cahuh! I'm sure you must be busy.*"

"*It's no bother at all Mr. Greig. To what honor do I owe the pleasure of your visit today?*" enquired the Governor in an overly deferent tone.

"*My Lord. I'll not waste your time. I've come as fast as I could from Marriaqua. A Carib neighbor of mine has this morning strongly advised me to withdraw myself from the island without delay. Cahuh-cahuh-cahuh! He said that it was the unanimous intention of the Black Caribs to soon declare war on the British. They plan to exterminate everyone, including women and children. Cahuh-cahuh-cahuh!*"[2]

"Are you certain of this Mr. Greig? There are presently so many wild rumors flying around the island it's hard for me sometimes to ascertain what's true," probed the Governor, giving Mr. Greig a moment to catch his breath.

"Aye Governor. His son is living in my household and we've been friends for almost ten years now. Cahuh-cahuh-cahuh! He gave me this warning out of kindness and concern for my safety," offered Mr. Greig earnestly as he fixed his unblinking gaze on the Governor. He continued to daub his sweat-covered forehead with his bloodied handkerchief as he spoke.

"I see. So, you believe this threat from the Black Caribs is credible?" asked the Governor with a skeptical, penetrating look in his eyes.

"Aye your excellency. That's why I came with all due haste to see you. Darn near killed my horse getting here. Poor Rollo nearly collapsed as we reached the top of Sion Hill,"[3] replied Mr. Greig in a woeful tone of voice.

"Gramercy. Thank you, Mr. Greig for your troubles. It is to great advantage that you've passed this information on to me so quickly."

He added cheerfully: "Please see Lieutenant George on your way out for some refreshment and a small token of the Crown's appreciation for your noble service in this regard."

With his last visitor dismissed, Governor Seton turned his attention to synthesizing all the information he had gathered that day. His mind instantly kicked into high gear. Assuming that the Black Caribs were unaware that their attack plans were exposed, he mused that this might offer the colonial forces a small window of opportunity which could be exploited to their advantage. He could try to stall for time to allow for reinforcements to arrive from Barbados or Martinique, by making diplomatic overtures to the Black Caribs. The Governor was also keenly aware that in the peace treaty from 1773 the Black Caribs were required to remain neutral in any conflict between France and Britain. He immediately sent a summons to several chiefs, including Chatoyé and Duvallé, requesting them to attend a council meeting in Kingstown the following Tuesday, as they had done on many previous occasions. Their response to his message would allow him to gauge their true intentions for war.

As an added precaution the Governor ordered all French settlers in the Colony, in particular those living on estates along the leeward coast, from Chateaubelair to Buccament, to declare their allegiance to the British Crown. Concomitantly, he issued an edict requiring them to turn in their weapons and corresponding ammunition within three days under penalty of incarceration. This would force them to remain neutral if a war broke out with France. No matter what would happen Governor Seton felt confident that he had done everything in his power to prepare for the Colony for the worst. He had acted swiftly and decisively in response to the threats at hand. This he believed would ensure there would be no chance of a repeat of what had occurred in Grenada and St Lucia under his command. It would only be a matter of time before his resolve would be put to the test.

PART II– Cry of Liberty

At length the hour of vengeance has arrived,
and the implacable enemies of the rights of man
have suffered the punishment due to their crimes.
My arm, raised over their heads,
has too long delayed to strike.
At that signal, which the justice of God has urged,
your hands, righteously armed,
have brought the axe upon the ancient tree of slavery and
prejudices.

(Jean-Jacques Dessalines - Excerpted from his proclamation to the Haitian people issued at Le Cap on 8th April 1804, entitled *'Liberty or Death' transcribed from "Orders issued by Dessalines, in the capacity of governor-general," The New Annual Register, or, General Repository of History, Politics, and Literature For the Year 1804 (1805):192-195.*)

CH9

~~~

Chief Chatoyé was alone in his hammock when the Governor's summons arrived. He usually took a nap after eating his midday meal. On this occasion, however, he had not managed to doze off, despite being weary from the previous night's ouïcou. His mind was flooded with thoughts about the imminent war. Strangely, he found himself, for the first time in his life, feeling apprehensive about going into battle. Perhaps it was because he was older and wiser than in the first war, a generation prior, when he was a younger, seemingly invincible warrior. Yet the churning in his gut was giving him a bad feeling despite the favorable omens divined by the boyez.

Lately, Chief Chatoyé could not seem to placate his maboyas nor please his ichéiri. No matter how many chickens he sacrificed or gris-gris that he wore around his arms and neck, his bad and good spirits were never satisfied. He wondered if the spirits had grown tired of the meagre drops of animal blood that they were offered and instead thirsted for luscious human blood. His ichéiri, his good spirits, had, as long as he could remember, always been very powerful. In fact, much stronger than his maboyas, his bad spirits. His ichéiri had protected him in combat on countless occasions from certain death and allowed him to evade severe injury. Yet now, it seemed as though they were weak and impotent, while his maboyas were gaining strength with each passing day, like the pressure building up in a volcano before it violently erupts. Secretly he worried if this could be the work of evil spirits acting on behalf of his enemies. Through the years he had accumulated many rivals, who he knew one day might seek revenge against him.

Chief Chatoyé left these uncomfortable thoughts behind as he made his way from Reuma's hut to the carbet in the center of Grand Sable to meet with Governor Seton's envoy. Several other chiefs had been summoned from the surrounding villages as well, so by the time he arrived, the carbet was already densely packed, with barely any standing room left. In fact, the whole of Grand Sable had seemingly turned out to get a glimpse of the peculiar white interloper. Chief Chatoyé could see Reuma and Ranné, along with several other women, loitering near the clump of annatto trees, with their reddish hairy fruit gleaming in the sunlight like fresh blood, a stone's throw away from the carbet. There they could conveniently observe everything that was taking place, while sitting in the shade.

As they looked on intently, the women gossiped and speculated about what was about to happen. To disguise their interest in such matters that were the traditional domain of Garifuna men, they kept themselves busy by flattening the heads of their infants.[1] Ignoring their protesting whimpers, they squeezed

66

their babies' heads as flat as possible between wooden boards pressed together by thin strips of cloth until the appropriate compression of their soft skulls was achieved. This seeming act of cruelty, was in fact borne out of deep maternal affection. Flat, backwards sloping foreheads were a sign of great beauty and perfection in Garifuna culture, which all mothers desired for their children. This was also presumed to be an advantage for their sons who would grow up one day to be warriors. It was widely believed that an arrow striking a flat forehead would bounce off and that flatter shaped heads were better at withstanding blows from boutous.

The Governor's aide-de-camp had been waiting impatiently for over an hour for the chiefs to assemble. He had arrived on horseback, dressed in his red and white ceremonial uniform, which was complimented with a sword sheathed in a silver scabbard that gleamed in the intense sunlight. Despite his impressive appearance, he looked pale and uneasy amongst the throng of Garifuna men. Beads of sweat trickled down his forehead profusely, giving it a clammy sheen. To pass the time he constantly fidgeted with the white-metal, brass buttons on his uniform, which made it clear that he couldn't wait to take it off. All of the men's eyes were fixated on his shiny scabbard, which was the talk of the carbet.

With the arrival of Chief Chatoyé along with the last remaining Garifuna chiefs, Lalime, Dufond and Massoteau, Chief

Joyette blew a lambis to bring the gathering to order. A hush fell over the men as Lieutenant George stepped forward and began reading the summons from Governor Seton in English:

Woyal subjects of da British Crown, on da authority granted to me by His Majesty, King George III, Sovereign rula of awl the Island of St. Vincent, as Gov'na of dis Cowony I sowemnly request awl Carib Chiefs and Signata's to da Angwo Carib Peace Treaty of 1773 to present demselves at a council meeting in Kingstown in three days to pwedge an Oath of Awegiance to da British Crown.[2] You are reminded dat in accordance wid da Treaty you are required to submit yourselves to da waws and obedience of his Majesty's govament, and furder dat no undue intacourse wid da French islands is awowed widout His Majesty's Gov'na's approbation. Refusal on your part to observe da conditions of da Treaty may be construed as a viowation of da Treaty concwuded between His Majesty and da Caribs.

Yours sincerely,
Gov'na of da Colony of St. Vincent,
His Excewency James Seton

As Lieutenant George finished reading Governor Seton's summons the blank looks on many chiefs' faces betrayed the fact that they had hardly comprehended what they had heard. As most of them were more comfortable in French than English due to their frequent intercourse with French smugglers from Guadeloupe, they had grasped only scattered fragments of the message.[3] Lieutenant George was therefore compelled to subsequently read a French translation of the summons, which had been prepared in anticipation of this eventuality.

With his duty completed, the Governor's aide-de-camp hastily made his way to his horse to head back to Kingstown. It seemed clear to him from the cold, emotionless expressions on the chiefs' faces that the Governor's message had not been well received. If he had to make a wager, he felt certain that it was unlikely that any of the chiefs would show up to meet the Governor in three days. Their body language communicated an intense hostility and aggression, which he sensed was directed towards himself as the conveyor of the Governor's threatening message. Or perhaps it was just a figment of his imagination. He had heard many a convincing rumor in Kingstown about how dangerous and violent the Black Caribs were; so he had already formed a bleak picture in his mind of what they were like, which colored his reading of the situation.

The chiefs were indeed not pleased with the Governor's message, however, for vastly different reasons than Lieutenant George could have imagined. After his departure a lively debate ensued in the carbet that lasted until sun down.

"*What king? We Garinagu are subjects of no one,[4] Not even France! We're citizens of a free nation! This blatant threat from the Governor demands a strong response!*" snarled Lalime, who often

69

spoke his mind bluntly and was prone to action before fully thinking matters through.

"*Yes brother. We should go to Kingstown to teach the Governor his place. Not take an oath to a king we've never seen. Such language shouldn't go unpunished!*" hissed Dufond, who frequently allied himself with his cousin Lalime. He possessed a temper like dry gunpowder, being always ready to fly off the handle at the slightest provocation. Despite his hotheadedness, Dufond was known to be a capable warrior, who was well respected by his fellow Garifuna tribesmen for his bravery in combat.

Chief Chatoyé, who had been listening intently and carefully weighing the implications of all that he had heard, then stepped in:

"*Brothers, your reasoning is sound and should indeed not go unheeded. Yet there's perhaps an even greater concern at play here. The Governor is requesting us to take this oath at a very critical moment in time. Just before we declare war. I suspect that the British may have already got wind of our impending attack. Going to Kingstown could be a way to lure us into a trap, like using pineapple to catch agouti.*"

"*I doubt the Governor has half a clue of what we're brewing here brother Chatoyé. We've only last night decided to take this action. Besides we've submitted oaths previously on several occasions. If we don't show up now wouldn't this betray our intentions?*" countered Lalime. Several of the assembled chiefs

70

nodded their heads in acknowledgement of Lalime's rational counterargument.

"*And what if brother Chatoyé is right? The timing of this summons is suspicious. If the Governor knows of our plans then we'd be fools to go to Kingstown,*" warned Massoteau, as he shot a supportive glance at Chief Chatoyé. He was a man of few words, but when he spoke he usually talked sense and everyone listened.

"*That's the point brothers. Our original plan was to begin the war when the new moon comes. But that'll surely give the British plenty of time to make defensive preparations and seek reinforcements. We must bring forward the start of our attack. It's the only way we can be certain to catch them off guard,*" argued Chief Chatoyé convincingly.

Looking into the disquieted eyes of the men, Chief Chatoyé continued in an even tone, "*The Governor will surely not take any action until the three-day period of the summons is past. So, we must strike before then.*"

"*I agree brother. This seems the most sensible course of action,*" concluded Joyette, who was impatient to reach a consensus and bring the discussion to a close so that he could go home for his evening meal. He looked around the carbet for a sign of dissent before stating with conviction, "*It's decided then. We commence our attack in three days' time!*" He added with a smirk directed at Dufond, "*Then you can show us all brother Dufond, how you'll teach Governor Seton his place!*"

71

Dufond responded to Joyette's insinuation with a truculent scowl, which made it clear that he intended to let his actions speak for themselves when the time came.

With the matter decided, all of the men present shook their heads in agreement and let out a chorus of ear-splitting war cries. *Ana, cariná rote! Only we are people! Ana, cariná rote! Only we are people! Ana, cariná rote! Only we are people!*

After the last cry, Chief Chatoyé added thoughtfully, "*We must notify our French allies of our change of plans and accelerate our preparations in the coming days.*"

He then brought the gathering to an abrupt close by issuing several orders in quick succession, "*Joyette, send word to the French about our revised plans. Lalime and Dufond, you are in charge of overseeing the weapons, ammunition and food stockpiles. I'll take care of sending Governor Seton a suitable response to his summons. We meet tomorrow to finalize the attack plans being drawn up by Duvallé. Let every moment count now brothers!*"

With those final words the men dispersed into the cool, early evening air. The women who had all the while been looking on from the patch of annatto trees, had heard the shrill war cries, immediately grasping their significance. They had already seen from a distance the fiery movements and violent gesticulations of the men during their heated debate. It was now certain beyond any shadow of doubt that war with the British was inexorable.

72

CH10

~~~

The sun had not long risen, yet Fort Charlotte was already buzzing with activity. A steady flow of militiamen, soldiers, merchants, vendors and slaves was trickling back and forth through the large, green, wrought iron gates marking the entrance to the redoubt on the summit of Berkshire Hill.[1] The aquamarine-colored watch tower, manned by two dragoons, could be seen peeking out conspicuously above the dull, grey limestone fortress walls signaling to everyone coming and going that they were under close scrutiny. Most impressive of all, to anyone who dared to cast a threatening gaze at the fortress, was its dizzying array of thirty-four artillery pieces of various calibers and ranges directed menacingly inland.[2]

As Governor Seton looked down from his perch atop the innermost rampart of the fort, near the watch tower, he had a breathtaking view of Bequia, the first of the chain of lush Grenadine islands snaking towards Grenada to the distant south. He shuddered in revulsion as his thoughts drifted momentarily to the unfortunate plight of Governor Home due to the insurrection raging there. Instinctively, his gaze shifted towards the windward direction, overlooking Kingstown harbor, until he finally settled on the endless stream of humanity pouring through the fort's gates.

The vendors and merchants could be seen zealously hawking their wares at the entrances to the barracks. Meanwhile the militiamen were busy conducting drills practicing marching in formation and simple defensive maneuvers. At the same time several dragoons with the help of a gang of male slaves were steadily restocking the armory with recently procured munitions, while still others were judiciously cleaning their muskets and the canons in preparation for combat. Everyone seemed to have found their place in the organized chaos that was Fort Charlotte.

The previous night had once again largely been uneventful in Kingstown. The Night Watch had only encountered a few drunken laggards who were summarily locked up for breaking curfew. However, in the Governor's household it had not been a serene night in the least. His wife, Susan, had become livid after discovering that his mistress, Josephine, had unashamedly moved her belongings into his sleeping chambers. This precipitated an embarrassing quarrel, punctuated by hysterical screams and violent sobbing from both women, which lasted well into the night. Governor Seton had therefore hardly slept a wink as he was temporarily forced to banish Josephine to the chamber-slaves' quarters to enforce a tenuous armistice with Susan. Josephine was most distraught by this decision and had to be unceremoniously dragged out, kicking and screaming, by his chamber slave, Koanda.

For his part, Koanda took no small pleasure in putting his hands on Josephine, as she had rejected his advances on several occasions in the past. Taking Josephine down a peg was all the more gratifying since she had become rather obnoxious in recent months, treating him and other servants in the Governor's household contemptuously, as if she herself was not descended from an African slave. In Koanda's mind it was long overdue that she was put in her rightful place.

The Governor's image of himself as a paragon of virtue was bruised by this incident since his wife swore on her mother's grave that she would write a letter to her wealthy family back in Scotland exposing his salacious affair. This imminent loss of face was most troubling to the Governor. However, he had hardly the time to dwell on it as he had other more pressing issues that were bedeviling him. Chief among them was the imminent threat of war with the Black Caribs and French. He was still awaiting a response from the Black Carib chiefs that he had summoned to meet him in two days' time. He hoped that this diplomatic gambit had bought the Colony sufficient time to secure its defenses.

This vortex of thoughts was engulfing Governor Seton's mind when Lieutenant George approached him.

"*Good morrow Gov'na. What a fine day it is!*"

"*Good morrow Lieutenant. The weather is indeed not half bad. How'd it go with your mission yesterday?*" The directness of the Governor's question made it clear that he was in no mood for chit chat.

"*Er, quite smoovly sir. I'd say it was manifestly a success,*" replied Lieutenant George casually, deliberately avoiding eye contact with Governor Seton as he spoke.

"*Do you reckon any of the Black Carib chiefs 'll show up on Tuesday?*" enquired the Governor as he searched his aide-de-camp's face for a more sincere answer.

"*I'm sure they'll do sir. Lord knows what'd happen if 'ey didn't. Dat'd be a right problem wouldn't it Gov'na?*" responded Lieutenant George, who was beginning to feel guilty for not sharing his honest assessment with the Governor. He was afraid to upset him, especially after the previous night's domestic drama with his wife and mistress, of which he did well to steer clear.

"*Most certainly it would Lieutenant! Otherwise, it would be a clear violation of the Treaty, which would have serious consequences.*"

After a brief pause the two men made a tour around the fort to inspect the defensive preparations being made, before taking midmorning tea.

As they were making their rounds, a tall, lanky man of middling age, with a thick mop of brown hair, accosted them. He was dressed in a Militia captain's uniform.

"*Governor Seton. Your Excellency may I steal a wee moment of your time?*" enquired the Militia Captain with an urgency in his voice.

"*Most certainly. What troubles you Captain? Is everything going well with the Militia's preparations?*" asked the Governor curiously.

"*Aye sir. All good so far. There is er... Well, you see sir I've just apprehended information that may prove most valuable to you... er I mean to our cause.*"

Pausing for a moment to gauge the level of interest he had aroused in the Governor, the Captain shot a probing look at the Governor as he continued:

"*A slave named Adam has, not half an hour ago, reported to me that he met last night with three Frenchmen in the company of several Carib men who offered to make him a chief.[3] They promised him epaulettes and his freedom if he could raise forty Blacks for their rebellious cause.*"

The Governor reflected thoughtfully on all that he had heard before replying evenly:

"*Gramercy. Thank you, Captain. This is indeed helpful information. We must certainly keep on guard for treacherous slaves. Those wretches can turn on us at any moment. I'll report this incident to Colonel Gordon and Major Lumsden later today when we meet to discuss the defense plans for Fort Charlotte.*"

Seeing an expectant gaze lingering in the Captain's eyes, the Governor hastily added, "*Lieutenant, please see to it that Captain, er...*"

"*Captain Alexander Leith sir, humbly at your service your Excellency.*"

"*That Captain Leith here receives a small token of appreciation from the Crown for his troubles.*" Patting him vigorously on the back, he added, "*Well done, lad!*"

Governor Seton then continued his strolling tour of Fort Charlotte alone, leaving Lieutenant George behind to sort the Captain out.

A few minutes later, he reached the armory where he was rejoined by the Lieutenant accompanied by a familiar-looking, middle-aged man wearing fine civilian clothing. By his self-assured strut and opulent style of dress the Governor quickly recognized the newcomer as the wealthiest man in the Colony, Sir William Young. Sir Young was of moderate height and possessed an innocent looking face, which was made slightly less cherubic by his bushy eyebrows and long pointy nose. On this occasion he was decked out in an ostentatious mustard-colored three-piece wool suit, composed of a lavishly embroidered cutaway tailcoat, waistcoat and breeches, trimmed with silk-cut black velvet. Perfectly matching the black trim of his tailcoat sleeves, were his low-heeled black leather shoes with large polished silver buckles, which contrasted delicately with his long white silk stockings.

78

Completing Sir Young's regal outfit, was a pleated white silk cravat wrapped impetuously around his neck, and a freshly pomaded and powdered, long curly, white-haired peruke.

Upon reaching the Governor's side, Lieutenant George made an obsequious, sweeping bow, before stepping forward to formally announce Sir Young to the Governor.

"Gov'na, I present to you Sir…"

Governor Seton cut him short by saying, *"S-Sir William Young, Good morrow to you my lord. How long has it been since our last meeting?"* The Governor spoke these words in an affable tone, as if he were meeting a long lost friend.

"Good morrow Governor. If memory serves me correctly it was at the Guy Fawkes ball last year at the Governor's Mansion."[4]

"Yes, that's right. It was a splendid evening wasn't it?"

"Most definitely Governor. Thou art a most generous host. And I must say an absolute paragon of class and virtue in the Colony."

The Governor blushed deeply in response to Sir Young's ingratiating compliment.

Sir Young paused for a moment to readjust his cravat with his right hand, before continuing:

"Unfortunately, your Excellency must forgive me, but today I've come to see you about matters that are far less pleasant."

"I see," replied Governor Seton soberly, while casting an searching gaze into Sir Young's eyes.

"Governor, Chief Chatoyé has asked me to convey a response to your summons on behalf of all the Black Carib chiefs."

Governor Seton's face became expressionless upon hearing these words, since he sensed that Sir Young was not about to share glad tidings. He was keenly aware that Sir Young enjoyed friendly relations with the foremost wild negro chief dating back to the signing of the treaty in 1773. Therefore, it came as no surprise that Sir Young was their chosen emissary.

"By all means my lord, please do continue," snapped the Governor with a slightly impatient air. He could already feel his temper beginning to boil up inside of him. However, he did his utmost to maintain his composure in the presence of his esteemed visitor.

Unruffled by the Governor's brusque tone, Sir Young continued:

"The Chiefs all honorably refuse to come to town this Tuesday on the grounds that it's now too late for such a meeting. They said that your message should've been sent much earlier.[5] The time for settling their grievances by words alone is long past."

The Governor's displeasure with the Black Caribs' message was written all over his thin, pasty face. His lips had become pursed and his eyes had narrowed, giving him a sour appearance.

"*Hmmmph. That's unfortunate to hear Sir Young. Such a violation of the Treaty indicates too clearly their intentions,*" sneered the Governor in a contemptuous tone.

"*I'm afraid so your Excellency. The good Lord knows I tried my best to dissuade Chief Chatoyé from this course of action. However, he said it's too late to change their minds. May God have mercy on us all.*"

Not desiring to extend the conversation further, the Governor hastily bid Sir Young farewell, before retiring to his office to ponder his next move. It was now clearer than ever that an insurrection was brewing in St. Vincent. The die was cast. Now all that could be done was to brace for the attack. Governor Seton sincerely hoped he had done enough to avert a calamity.

CH11

~~~

A fog of tranquility hung in the cool morning air, like a mist hovering over the rainforest at dawn, as Warramou and Duvallé made their way, from Owia to the carbet in Grand Sable. As they walked in single file along the cragged, winding path straddling the windward coast both men kept silent. Each man was trapped deep within his own thoughts and avoided disturbing the other with idle chatter.

Duvallé was preoccupied with the attack plans, which he was incessantly turning over in his mind to ensure that no small detail had been overlooked. He knew in the marrow of his bones that any miscalculation would have dire consequences for the Garifuna. The gravity of this fact was not lost on him. Yet a small fragment of doubt was slowly creeping into his thoughts, and gnawing away at his confidence. He suppressed it immediately, knowing full well that hesitation would only bedevil the plans he had hatched. Nothing good could come of such indecisive thinking at this stage. The point of no return had long been reached.

Warramou, for his part, was already engorged on the adrenaline coursing through his veins, fueled by his anticipation of the imminent commencement of hostilities. This made it impossible for him to focus his mind for long before it would dart off impulsively jumping from one sporadic thought to the next. Wielding his prized boutou savagely in combat, smearing his face with red war paint made from crushed annatto seeds, making poison-tipped arrows by dipping the sharp edges of the arrowheads in toxic milky-white Manchineel sap, Ranné's infectious smile melting his heart, the intoxicating mineral smell of Lorain's fresh blood mingled with sweat and charred earth, the suffocating sulfuric odor of gunpowder and burnt flesh hanging in the air, the delicious aroma of freshly baked ereba dipped in spicy tumallen sauce – all of these disparate thoughts were churning in his head. At the same time, he could feel pangs of malaise welling in his gut which portended something far more profound than he could apprehend from the jumbled mosaic of his mind.

Chief Chatoyé, Massoteau, Dufond, Joyette, Lalime, and Citoyen Touraille, along with one of his French lieutenants, Citoyen Mather,[1] were already at the carbet, engrossed in intense discussion in French, when the two men arrived.

"So, you see, we must strike right away lest we lose the advantage that we've obtained at the moment. As you're undoubtedly aware, the British are presently indisposed to fight and their defenses are undermanned."

It was Chief Chatoyé, who was calmly reiterating the need for a pre-emptive strike against the British.

"What you say is unquestionably true my dear General. Yet I beg your indulgence to consider if we'd better serve our purpose

83

by waiting for reinforcements to arrive from Guadeloupe before commencing our attack? This would necessarily permit us to have a more formidable fighting force with which to crush the British just like we did in Guadeloupe six months ago," countered Citoyen Touraille, who was eager to show that, despite his youthful appearance, he could hold his own against a veteran warrior like Chief Chatoyé, when it came to military strategy.

"*The latest information that we've received from Governor Hugues is that the invasion force'll be ready to set sail from Guadeloupe in four days' time, after reinforcements arrive from France. So, they'll reach St Vincent a day or two later depending on the weather,*" added Citoyen Touraille with conviction, despite the fact that he knew that what he was saying was hardly assured.

"*Unfortunately, time does not afford us such luxury my dear revolutionary brother. Duvallé has devised a new plan accounting for the present circumstances, which permits us to exploit the enemy's present weakness,*" responded Chief Chatoyé, unfazed by Citoyen Touraille's challenge. He cast a sharp glance towards his brother, Duvallé, urging him to elaborate further.

"*We'll divide our forces into two armies. One commanded by Chief Chatoyé composed of a mix of Garifuna warriors and Frenchmen, which will sweep down the leeward side of the island.*[2] *And I'll lead the second army made up of Garifuna warriors and slaves. We'll come down the windward coast,*" explained Duvallé as he drew a rough outline of Hiroona in the sandy earth of the carbet floor with a twig. As he spoke about each army's attack route he indicated it on the crude map.

"*Massoteau, Dufond and Warramou, you'll be my lieutenants. Joyette, Lalime and Citoyen Touraille you'll be Chief Chatoyé's seconds,*" added Duvallé finally, while looking at each man in turn as he spoke his name, to confirm his assignment.

"*And what about the French Revolutionary Army that'll soon be on its way from Guadeloupe to second the brave Black Charaibes?*" enquired Citoyen Touraille, who was concerned that the pivotal role of the French revolutionaries was being overlooked in Duvallé's plan.

"*They'll intersect us at Kingstown harbor, and then together we'll massacre all the British on the island,*" calmly replied Duvallé, who had accounted for every eventuality in his planning.

"*Bravo! Bravo! So that leaves just one final question: When are we going to launch the firs' attaque?*" asked Citoyen Mather with a curious glint in his eyes. His thick, guttural Gardois jabber made him slightly incomprehensible.

"*Tonight at first moonlight,*" announced Duvallé triumphantly. After seeing the Frenchmen's raised eyebrows, he added, "*However, Chief Chatoyé's leeward army won't deploy till tomorrow morning. Will that work for you and your men?*"

The Frenchmen's eyes lit up with delight.

"*Yes of course! The men have been itching for a fight since getting here. We stand at the ready to heed your smallest* command," offered Citoyen Touraille emphatically, adding *"Citoyen Mather and I'll inform the men right away."*

"Very well," confirmed Chief Chatoyé with a cheerful smile, *"See you at the rendezvous point in Grand Sable at daybreak,"* as he bid them farewell.

With the departure of the Frenchmen, Chief Chatoyé and Duvallé turned their attention to checking on the final preparations for the war. They had intentionally avoided sharing details about the strength and disposition of the Garifuna fighting force in the presence of their French allies since this was closely guarded information, to which no European was privy. Dufond, Massoteau, Lalime and Warramou in the coming day would make several caches of munitions and provisions at various strategic points along the planned attack routes to ensure smooth logistics. These stores would be indicated by markings on trees and rocks which were only discernible to the keen eyes of Garifuna warriors. In addition, the men would also stash several canoes and pirogues at a few inlets along the windward coast to sustain their smuggling links to Karukera, Hewanorra and Camerhogne which would be a vital lifeline if the war did not reach a quick resolution. Confident that everything was in order the men dispersed to have a last meal with their wives and children, before taking a rest in anticipation of the night's looming action.

Warramou headed back alone, towards Uwamá's hut, however, he felt unhinged. His mind was still reeling with an

86

uncontrollable gyre of thoughts. To calm his jangled nerves, he made a small detour up the mountain side, in the direction of Mount Qualibou, to visit the giant Buffalo tree in the nearby woods. This verdant tree marked the burial site of his grandfather, *Pa Louen*.[3] The spirits of the ancestors were often believed to inhabit these mystical trees in the afterlife.[4] Warramou always consulted his deceased grandfather on seminal occasions such as these. Reaching out his right hand to clasp the wavy, thick, elephant trunk-like roots of the tree, he sang a cappella an aromakani, a sacred traditional song, asking *Pa Louen* for spiritual guidance and strength in the upcoming war:[5]

> *"Oh, will you be my guide in this world?*
> *Oh, give me your strength my companion in truth,*
> *Oh, let's go see the Masters of the world,*
> *What shall we say to them?*
> *What shall we say to them?*
> *The sun beats down on my soul."*

After Warramou finished singing he turned around and slowly sauntered away. With each step, he felt his mental haze beginning to clear. In its wake a singular realization emerged, which allayed the qualms that had been stirring in his bowels all day. This war was about more than just Garifuna freedom from British hegemony. It was ultimately about the survival of their way of life in Hiroona. It would be a war they could not afford to lose.

87

CH12

~~~

The gibbous moon slipped behind a cloud, momentarily casting a blanket of darkness over the night sky. Without hesitation Chief Duvallé gave the signal his lieutenants had been eagerly awaiting. *Quaw quaw quaw. Scree ree lee.*[1] Seconds later a lone flaming arrow streaked across the sky before being swallowed up by the void of darkness making the ground and sky indistinguishable. This was soon followed by a volley of more than a dozen flaming arrows which briefly illuminated the heavens until they vanished like the first arrow into the sea of murk.

As the moon reemerged the yellow and orange glow of the burgeoning flames could be seen rapidly spreading through the sugarcane fields surrounding the La Croix estate,[2] accompanied by billows of sweet, noxious smoke. Soon after, several men and women could be seen frantically running from the plantation buildings with pails of water in a vain attempt to contain the fire, hopelessly unaware of their impending doom. Duvallé's men, who were lurking in the brush, had completely encircled the estate, owned by Madame La Croix, a well-known French settler with pro-British sympathies, cutting off any chance of escape. However, they did not yet draw their noose tighter, preferring instead to bide their time until the moment was ripest. This soon presented itself as the conflagration consumed field after field of nearly full-grown sugar cane, leaving only two possible paths of flight for the inhabitants of the estate. Both leading to their demise.

When the moon vanished once more, Chief Duvallé gave the signal for the onslaught to begin in earnest. He let out an ear-splitting war cry, *Ana, cariná rote! Only we are people!,* which was soon echoed by nearly two hundred Garifuna fighters brandishing cutlasses, *boutous,* spears, knives and muskets, as they hurled themselves towards the plantation, situated in a shallow, fertile vale. *Ana, cariná rote! Only we are people! Ana, cariná rote! Only we are people! Ana, cariná rote! Only we are people!* These deafening ululations sent shivers down the spines of the estate's inhabitants, causing them to shriek in fear, abandoning their firefighting efforts to desperately seek refuge and armament. But it was too late. Hordes of fighters were already descending upon the plantation compound in vicious waves obliterating anything and anyone crossing their path.

The first victim, a middle-aged Irish overseer, was pursued like a bloodhound by Massoteau. He wielded a long knife in his left hand and a tomahawk in the other, which he used to viciously hack at the overseer's right arm as he grasped the iron bracket of the door to the horse stables, in a futile attempt to escape. Massoteau then savagely stabbed and cut him in the back and neck, until his lifeless body fell to the ground at his feet. As he withdrew his knife from the corpse he felt an exhilarating surge of adrenaline shooting through his veins. This was intensified further by the intoxicating, mineral aroma of fresh blood that flooded his senses, causing his nostrils to flare and his eyes to bulge with drunken bloodlust. Wiping his knife and tomahawk clean on the overseer's trousers he then scanned the darkness for another target. Moments later, he found his next victim, a pubescent slave boy armed with a machete, hiding in one of the stables. Massoteau ensured that in short order, he met a similar fate as the overseer.

However, the bloodletting was only just beginning. Duvallé together with a dozen men unleashed their rabid fury on the main plantation Great House after drawing several sporadic bursts of musket fire from its vicinity. With little effort they infiltrated its barricaded mahogany doors using their cutlasses and spears, before proceeding to cut down every living being that they encountered. They rampaged from room to room satisfying their thirst for blood by bashing in skulls and chopping off limbs left and right. Women and children, master and slave, no one was spared their ferocious wrath. Many of their victims were found on their knees saying their prayers, pleading for God's mercy while imploring their assailants to spare them. Yet it was in vain. The dam of pent-up frustration and resentment towards the British, that had festered in the twenty years since the last war, had burst and was being unleashed all at once. After ransacking the Great House's contents, they set it ablaze before moving onto the overseer's house and slave quarters.

Warramou also got in on the action despite being on the tail end of the first wave of fighters. He had stopped dead in his tracks after spotting movement in a bush out of the corner of his eye. As other fighters had stampeded past he decided to take a closer look. Strangely, at that moment it did not occur to him that he should be particularly cautious as he approached the bush. He was lulled into a state of overconfidence by the ease with which Duvallé's army was overrunning the estate. So he walked with his boutou hanging down loosely at his side and with his dagger sheathed in his loincloth. He squinted his eyes as he ambled towards the bush trying to discern what he had seen. When he was within ten paces of the scrub, to Warramou's surprise, a bare-chested, adolescent female slave with short cropped hair and dark ebony skin, rushed out at him wielding a long, sharp implement in her right hand, which she flailed wildly in the air.

When she reached within arm's length she made a sudden lunging movement at Warramou in an attempt to stab him in the abdomen. Out of pure reflexive instinct he stepped backwards and seized his boutou firmly with both hands, lifting it upwards to protect himself. The young slave woman then unflinchingly, pressed home her advantage by sidestepping as she hurled herself towards him, before cleanly delivering a slashing blow across his ribs. Warramou bit his tongue as he swallowed the pain that was violently welling up in him as blood slowly began to ooze from his right side.

Quickly, he came to his senses. Using his boutou he repaid his adversary with a solid crack on the forehead. The rush of pain surging through her skull momentarily stunned her, while at the same time violently infuriating her. The young slave woman became more aggressive and dangerous like a wounded manicou. Over and over again she charged at Warramou, each time almost succeeding in evading his defenses. As she huffed and puffed preparing for another vicious attack, Warramou addressed her in French:

"You are a feisty one aren't you. Where'd you learn to fight like that?"

She spat on the ground in response.

"Well, I guess you need another taste of my boutou don't you?"

She snorted and let out a loud grunt as she rushed towards him again. This time she feigned going to the right then ducked sharply to the left as she delivered a slanting cut dangerously close to his manhood, which grazed his left thigh.

In retaliation, he rewarded her with two solids thumps on the crown of her head in quick succession.

She stumbled to right but soon managed to recover her balance.

He yelled at her furiously, *"That's enough now! I'm done playing around with you woman!"*

She smirked ominously as she prepared for another charge. This time, however, Warramou was alert to her cunning. He read her every move and knocked her weapon cleanly away. It sailed through the air, ending up far out of her reach.

Startled, they both measured each other for a moment, before the young slave woman finally broke her silence.

"*Gowan den. What yo waitin' fo? Ain't yo man 'nuff to kill a wohman?*"

Warramou fixed his gaze assiduously on her in response. Till then he had hardly took notice of the appearance of his foe. For a moment, his eyes drank her in slowly from head to toe. In the wavering firelight, he could make out her handsome, round face with full lips and slightly protruding eyes which peeked out from under her sharply arched eyebrows, endowing her with a defiant yet regal disposition. She was of moderate height and possessed a shapely form, which was accentuated slightly by her narrow waist and knock-knees. It was also plain for Warramou to see that her sinewy frame was hewn from years of toiling in the fields.

Under Warramou's intense, piercing gaze the young slave woman became self-conscious and instinctively looked away from him.

Warramou blushed as he struggled to find his tongue.

"I-I could end this right now you know. But what's the point of taking your life senselessly? Our quarrel is not with your people anyway."

Pausing briefly to marshal his thoughts, he added, "If you surrender now I give you my word no harm shall come to you."

After an awkward pause in which she seemed to weigh his words carefully in her mind, he ventured, "Your fighting skills are impressive sister. We could definitely put you to good use in this war we are fighting against the British."

Yet she remained silent in response.

He changed tack to see if it would elicit a reaction from her.

"I'm Warramou. Second lieutenant of Chief Duvallé, commander of the windward Garifuna army. At your service. What's your name sister?" enquired Warramou with a curious glint in his eyes.

She studied him cautiously, as if she was unsure whether he could be fully trusted, before answering, "I'm Nanette. But 'roun hey dey does call me Nan."

"Well Nan, are you perhaps interested in joining our cause to drive the British out of Hiroona?"

"I s'pose so Mistah Warramou. As long I's free and yo ain't go sen' me go back."

In the back of her mind Nanette was worried about being resold into slavery by the Black Caribs. This fate had befallen many runaway slaves, including her mother. At her previous

94

planation in Barrouallie, Nanette had been distressed after witnessing her mother receive one hundred and fifty lashes for her third escape attempt. The skin on her mother's buttocks, thighs and back had been shredded into large welts, which remained raw for several months. For good measure, to prevent her from ever contemplating absconding again, the cruel slave master, had thereafter locked her mother up for a week in the 'hotbox', stark-naked without any covering for her wounds. With hardly any food and water, her mother had almost expired from the brutal trifecta of dehydration, starvation and ulceration from her festering wounds. Hence, Nanette was keen to ensure that this would not be her fate if she capitulated. She would rather die than be enslaved again.

"Don't worry Nan. You're free and we won't sell you back to the British. If you fight on our side your liberty will be assured for the rest of your days," added Warramou with a reassuring smile.

In the meantime, the commotion of the battle around them had subsided. Duvallé's army had succeeded in brutally crushing all resistance at the La Croix estate. It had been a comprehensive slaughter. In the aftermath, all that remained were a handful of slave women and their children, amongst the smoldering ashes of charred sugar cane and human flesh, which filled the air with a sweetly acrid stench. The first engagement of the war had gone according to plan, yet a long road still lay ahead before they would reach the British bastion of Kingstown.

CH13

~~~

That same night, a contingent from the Militia, stationed near the outermost limits of Kingstown along the windward coast, set out on patrol. Their mission on this occasion was to investigate the bizarre report of a local resident who claimed he had seen balls of fire streaking across the sky earlier in the evening.[1] Although it seemed outlandish at the time, the Militia party was nevertheless sent out to search the nearby woods. It would at the very least help them to pass the time while they waited anxiously for the first action of the war to begin. Led by the clever yet inexperienced Captain Alexander Leith, the detachment of twenty-five men, ventured boldly forth despite being only lightly armed with a handful of muskets and machetes between them. Due to the dense brush, they walked in Indian file, in complete silence, guided by a hooded lantern, and the light of the waning moon, which was obscured intermittently by the forest canopy and light cloud cover.

Alexander had a hunch that they might be able to gather some useful intelligence on the Black Caribs and their French allies, which he hoped to pass onto Governor Seton for another small reward. After much haggling with the Governor's aide-de-camp, he had received a measly half-crown's compensation for his earlier tip, which had hardly helped to ease his financial straits.

He was heavily indebted to several people, including the tavern owner and Rosie, his slave mistress, due to his lifestyle of constant dissipation.

Unlike many of his fellow militiamen, he was eagerly looking forward to the start of hostilities since he had a premonition that the war would herald a change in his fortune. All he needed to do was to play his cards right and suppress his compulsions, at least for the time being. He was keenly aware that his proclivity for drink, gambling and women were his downfall. So he had resolved to himself to not touch a drop of liquor or enter a brothel or gambling den until the war campaign was concluded.

As the men ambled along slowly, wading their way through the dense brush, Alexander lost himself in reverie. He fantasized about being decorated by the Governor with a medal of valor after emerging victoriously from a fierce battle that had resulted in dozens of enemy fatalities. In this vivid daydream he imagined himself as the leader of a company of militiamen in the defense of a strategic position, situated on a hill, which was facing a crushing assault. What had saved the day was his brilliant leadership at a critical juncture during the battle when their position was nearly overrun. He had ordered his men to fire off a round of grapeshot at close range against a surging mass of enemy infantrymen with bayonets fixed, who were charging their position.[2] This had wiped out the entire front wave of the attack, stalling the enemy's assault. As a result, precious time was gained for reinforcements in the form of Dragoons to arrive, who had turned the tide of the battle in their favor in the nick of time.

Just as he was about to dive deeper into another one of his heroic fantasies, a faint murmur in the distance yanked Alexander back to reality. As they drew closer, the noise became more distinct. He could make out the sound of drums accompanied by a cacophony of strident voices. Before long, a dim shaft of light could be seen filtering through the trees, leading to a clearing. Alexander's heart began to race ecstatically. He held his right palm up, giving the signal for his men to halt and extinguish the lantern. For a moment they waited in the dark allowing their eyes to adjust to the dimness, while listening to the commotion up ahead. It sounded like raucous, drunken singing in French and Carib.

They did not know it at the time, but their patrol had stumbled upon an ouïcou celebrating the victory of Duvallé's army hours earlier at the La Croix estate.[3] As was customary, the festivities lasted deep into the night and were well lubricated with tafia, guifiti, cassava beer and wine. The music and dancing were in full swing by the time the Militia party arrived on the scene.

Sensing their good fortune, Alexander instructed his men to stealthily fan out among the foliage surrounding the clearing. Given their light armament, as well as uncertainty over the strength of the enemy forces and the terrain, he prudently opted for caution before launching an attack. He knew that the element of surprise would only be a momentary advantage, which could

98

quickly be compensated by a superior force. Despite this fact, even if he did not admit it to himself at the time, the prospect of returning to base without engaging the enemy was not an option that crossed his mind. His chief concern was in fact how to achieve this objective while ensuring the safety of himself and his men.

As Alexander bided time sussing out the situation, a young Frenchman took leave of the festivities and headed towards the bushes. He staggered left and then right as he moved unsteadily towards the darkness enveloping the periphery of the clearing, oblivious to the danger that lay in wait. After stumbling, and almost falling over twice, he pulled out his member and began to void, letting out a low moan of satisfaction as he relieved himself. In a flash, Alexander extended the muzzle of his musket from the dark bowels of the bush, and pressed it against the Frenchman's temple. As he did so Alexander motioned, with his right index finger to his lips, for the Frenchman not to make a sound. Adding in a whispery voice, *"One wee move and I'll put some lead betwixt your ears."*

Inebriated and caught off-guard the Frenchman had no choice but to comply. He was quickly relieved of a knife that hung loosely around his waist along with a leather poire-poudre full of gunpowder.[4] Two militiamen then seized him by both arms and bound his limbs with cord while stuffing his mouth with an old muslin rag. Realizing that the Frenchman would soon be missed by his comrades, Alexander plucked up the courage to give the order for his men to launch the attack. He gave the signal by screaming his clans' battle cry, *Buaidh no bàs! Victory or death!*[5]

Alexander's rallying cry was drowned out by the loud merrymaking of the revelers who were almost all in an advanced state of intoxication. Thus, several precious moments were lost by the French and Black Carib carousers before they realized what was happening. In their confusion, as would later be recounted to Chief Chatoyé, several men in fact had haplessly continued their dancing and singing. While others, who had swiftly perceived the danger, raised an alarm as they fled into the darkness in every direction possible, like cockroaches scattering in the light.

Miraculously, in the chaos that ensued, Alexander's men succeeded in taking only a handful of revelers prisoner.[6] This was due in no small part to the militiamen's healthy respect for the Black Caribs' combat skills in close quarters, which were widely feared. Many of them in truth considered the Militia detachment's rather light armament to be inadequate to the task of subduing such fearsome adversaries. This invariably led them to dither, resulting in a halfhearted charge which allowed their quarry to slip away into the night. Although, it should be noted that in Alexander's subsequent relation of this event to his superiors, he made no mention of this hesitancy on the part of his men. Instead, he expounded hyperbolically on the overwhelming odds with which he and his men had been confronted, highlighting in particular how they had prevailed unscathed despite fierce

100

resistance. In some versions of this story, Alexander would even claim that they were outgunned and outnumbered by a factor of no less than three or four to one, in his estimation. Naturally, this pushed the boundaries of credulity since not a single shot had been fired on either side, nor were any casualties recorded.

The news of the Militia's interception of enemy forces on the previous night's patrol sent shockwaves through the small community of planters on the windward side of the island as they awoke. They needed no further confirmation that the war was at their doorstep. This prompted many of them to flee forthwith in panic. By mid-morning caravans of planters, with their wives, children and slaves were streaming along the main highway towards Kingstown. Many of them had only the clothes on their backs and a few meagre possessions that they could carry with them. Silverware and other valuables which they could not easily transport had been hastily buried prior to their departure. Some planters had even left some of their slaves behind to look after their plantations, albeit with no arms to protect themselves against the vagaries of Duvallé's marauding Black Carib army.

Governor Seton reacted swiftly upon hearing the alarming report about the Militia's apprehension of foreign agents on Vincentian soil. He immediately declared war against the French and Black Caribs, before dispatching a heavily armed commando of sixty horsemen to bolster the Militia's ranks on the windward coast. He hoped the latter would help to intercept any enemy assault that might come towards Kingstown from that direction. He also put the defensive forces at Fort Charlotte on high alert in anticipation of an impending attack. The war had finally begun. It would not take long for the full extent of the threat to the Colony's continued existence to become clear.

CH14

~~~

At first light, the vicious rampage of the Garifuna forces continued unabated. Duvallé's army swept inexorably down the windward coast from the Carib boundary to the Yambou River, savagely extirpating every fragment of the British presence in Hiroona that crossed its path. In its wake it left a devastating trail of death and destruction. The countryside was littered with dozens of bloodied corpses of the British and their sympathizers. It was as if a cloud of death was diffusing, slowly smothering the island. Yet this was merely the residual of the pent-up wrath of the Garifuna, which continued to surge uncontrollably like a flooded river bursting its banks. Not even the British cattle were spared their ire, let alone their landed property. No fewer than thirty sugar works and cane fields had been set alight leaving behind an unmistakable haze of grey and black smoke blanketing the sky. The smoke plumes, visible for miles around, spread out ominously above the sharply rising hills and undulating valleys of the island, appearing like seams of blackened blood gushing forth from a giant gaping wound in the heart of the verdant landmass.

By midmorning Duvallé's forces had cut a large swathe through the windward territory and were rapidly progressing southwards towards Calliaqua, when they encountered their first pocket of resistance. A heavily armed commando of three score men, some riding on horseback, had advanced towards them via the main highway from Kingstown.[1] Initially, on the offensive, the British had opened fire wounding several Garifuna warriors on the frontline. Among them was Dufond who was shot in the thigh, while attempting to attack the enemy's flank. He narrowly avoided a worse fate thanks to the fortuitous arrival of a sizeable body of Garifuna warriors which swarmed to his aid and that of their fallen comrades. Quickly realizing that they were vastly outnumbered, the commando turned to flight. In the ensuing frantic retreat, the British suffered no fewer than a dozen casualties from the flood of poison-tipped arrows and musket-fire that rained unrelentingly down upon them as they fled. The survivors were lucky to escape with their lives and limbs intact as they beat a hasty retreat to the safety of Kingstown.

Later that day, near the Massarica river, Duvallé's army again clashed with the enemy.[2] A company of militiamen and volunteers, some on foot and some on horseback, had marched out to the meet them. Duvallé cunningly ordered his men to wave their turbans at the British in friendship. As they drew closer, however, he gave a signal for a detachment of his men concealed behind a felled silk-cotton tree to open fire with their muskets. This proved lethally effective as a score of British combatants fell dead in their tracks. The survivors wisely opted to hastily retreat towards Kingstown taking great care to avoid the main highway to town which had become a death trap due to the marauding bands of Garifuna warriors entrenched in the area. To preserve themselves, many stragglers took circuitous routes to town after hiding out for hours in the surrounding cane fields. Several of them narrowly evaded capture, as they were hunted ruthlessly like wild game, by packs of bloodthirsty Garifuna. In fact, they were the lucky ones, as the wounded received no quarter. Their arms and legs were hacked off, before their throats were slit silencing their futile pleas for compassion.

Meanwhile, on the leeward coast Chatoyé's army was making equally rapid progress, albeit less destructively. Unlike Duvallé, Chief Chatoyé chose to leave most of the plantations he encountered intact, reserving his fury instead for the British settlers and their partisans, to whom he showed no mercy. As he led a joint force composed of French revolutionaries and French settlers with their slaves, the plantations of the French inhabitants on the western half of the island were left largely unmolested. Being an astute leader, Chief Chatoyé also realized that leaving these properties intact would be beneficial once the Garifuna and French had prevailed in the war.

At Richmond's Estate, just south of the Wallilabou River, Chatoyé's army briefly paused it's lightning advance towards Chateaubelair, the northernmost European settlement on the leeward coast of the island. Seeking replenishment, his men ransacked and pillaged the plantation. During their search for

105

nourishment, munitions and plunder they discovered a Scottish estate manager, one Mr. Kearton,[3] cowering in a shallow pit beneath the floorboards of a barn. In short order, he was brought before Chief Chatoyé for an appropriate punishment to be meted out.

As a man of honor and justice, Chief Chatoyé, consulted a group of newly freed slaves from the estate prior to passing judgement.

"Free brothers and sisters, I seek your council in deciding this man's fate. No doubt remains in my mind that he has inflicted great suffering upon you. What do you wish to be done with him?"

A chorus of furious voices eagerly answered, *"Burn 'im at da stake! Boil 'im in molasses! Run 'im tru' da rollas!"*

The estate manager turned pale upon hearing his impending doom. He began to shake uncontrollably while sweating profusely in panic. Reluctant to accept his fate, he shamelessly resorted to pleading for leniency.

Getting down on both knees and clasping his shackled hands together as if he was about to pray, he groveled, *"I humbly beseech your Excellency's clemency. Please God save me! I beg your mercy o' great noble chief."*

Chief Chatoyé's eyes narrowed and his brow furrowed as he cast a disapproving frown at the estate manager while again asking the crowd of freed slaves gathered around him, *"Tell me, what shall this coward's fate be?"* The scornful expression written
106

on his face made it plain for all to see that he found Mr. Kearton's plea for leniency, pathetic and unbecoming of a man.

This time the mob screamed even more fervently, *"Burn 'im at da stake! Boil 'im in molasses! Run 'im tru' da rollas! Run 'im tru' da rollas! Run 'im tru' da rollers! Massa day dun!"* With each punishment, their voices grew more strident, until they reached a fever pitch.

Chief Chatoyé nodded solemnly in approval and without blinking an eye or showing any emotion, ordered the estate manager's execution, *"Mr. Kearton, by the power vested in me as commander of this revolutionary army, I hereby condemn you to death for your vile crimes against the people of Hiroona. Take him to the cane mill and run him through the cylinders!"*

Pandemonium erupted amongst the former slaves, whose faces were all beaming with satisfaction at the verdict. As he was led away in chains to face his death sentence, amid a sea of lude jeers and taunts, the estate manager burst into tears, while letting out an ear-piercing wail. He cried out bitterly, *"I curse you and your children and your children's children. You'll all rot in hell for this! The lot of you savages!"*

Not long after, Mr. Kearton's bloodcurdling screams could be heard echoing across the plantation yard, as Chief Chatoyé's army prepared to push on in their conquest of the leeward coast. The bloodletting in Hiroona was far from over.

By nightfall Chateaubelair was in Chatoyé's hands. Along the way his joint French-Garifuna army had seized a strip of territory extending all the way from Etherington Bay in the far north, down through the Grand Bonhomme Mountains in the center of the island, to the banks of the Troumaca River. In the span of less than a day, more than half of Hiroona lay under the control of the Garifuna and their allies. Till then their armies had not yet been fully tested in combat as they had faced anemic resistance in their southward advance. Most settlers had opted to flee to Kingstown rather than to stay and defend their property. Governor Seton's calculus had not accounted for their protection. Kingstown had been his main focus while the countryside had been sacrificed. Soon the Governor's desperate gamble would be put to the test.

CH15

~~~

The pungent odor of dank, moss-covered limestone filled the air as a heavy downpour drenched Fort Charlotte at dawn. The nauseating, moldy smell reeked of death and decay, making Josephine cough softly as she awoke. She rolled over in bed and rested her head affectionately on Governor Seton's hairy chest listening to the steady lubdub of his heart as he slept. She was relieved to have found her way back into his loving arms after her banishment the previous nights. He had easily succumbed when she crept into his chambers after she was certain that his wife had retired to her quarters for the night. The Governor had weakly protested at first but did not repel her when her hands slipped adeptly under his nightshirt and brought his manhood to life.

As Josephine lay awake she dreamed of leaving the tropics and venturing to the Governor's native Scotland, where he had promised to take her one day. Unlike her former French lover, who had once made a similar vow, the Governor had the means and power to give her the refined life that she felt she deserved. Having witnessed the hardship and suffering of her mother as a wretched field slave, Josephine was adamant that she would not end up like her. At all costs she was determined to elevate her station in life. For this reason, she had conveniently ignored the fact that the

Governor was married and justified her betrayal of the confidence of his wife, Susan, for whom she had served as a chambermaid for over a year. In her mind, it was a necessary evil in order to get what she wanted. That was just how life was. The only way to get what you want was to take it, by force if necessary. The strong always prevailed over the weak. Josephine had even convinced herself that the Governor truly loved her and would do anything she demanded to please her. After this infernal war was over, she was certain that he would abandon his wife and finally take her to his faraway homeland. She dreamed of living in a stately Scottish mansion with a well-manicured lawn, and attending elegant aristocratic balls draped in the latest high fashion from Europe.

As if he heard her thoughts, Governor Seton opened his eyes and lovingly stroked the small of her back with the palm of his pale, spindly hand.

"You're up early my princess. What's the matter?"

She answered by kissing him tenderly on the lips and pressing her supple bosom against his bushy chest.

"You surprised me by coming last night." His soft but firm tone of voice conveyed a mild admonishment.

"I couldn't resist any longer James. It was too much to bear. You can't imagine what it's like staying in those dreadful chamber slave quarters!" She pleaded with him although she knew that she had already won his tacit approval for her to remain in his bedchamber.

110

"*You know I can't live without you Josephine.*"

"*I forgive you. But I can't go back. You understand that don't you James. I just can't.*"

Josephine fell silent, with her soft lips gently caressing the nape of the Governor's neck. At that moment there was an urgent knock on the door.

The Governor at first ignored it and refused to get up as he basked in the warmth of Josephine's embrace. However, the persistence of the knock eventually forced him to his feet. He approached the door sullenly and without opening it grumpily demanded, "*Who dares to disturb me at this ungodly hour? If this isn't about a pressing matter I'll have you flogged forthwith.*"

"*Good morrow Gov'na! Sorry to… er disturb you sir. Very urgent news has arrived dat can't wait,*" replied Lieutenant George, somewhat hesitantly. He had deduced from the marked irritation in the Governor's tone of voice, that the Governor was not alone.

After hastily donning his long, off-white linen nightshirt and cloaking himself with his blue, woolen formal jacket, Governor Seton emerged into the small anteroom to his bedchamber, discretely closing the door behind him.

"*What's this all about Lieutenant? Surely this news could wait.*"

As if to justify the exigency of his intrusion, Lieutenant George triumphantly blurted out, "*Chateaubewair has fawen sir!*"

111

The look of shock etched on the Governor's face nakedly expressed his disbelief in what he had just heard.

Nodding his head in confirmation, Lieutenant George added, "*Yes Gov'na. It's true. Word arrived not wong ago dat da rebels seized Chateaubewair yesterday evening.*"

"*B-but how could that be Lieutenant? I-I sent a strong Militia detachment to reinforce our position there two days ago.*"

The Governor spoke these last words to absolve himself of responsibility for what had happened in Chateaubelair. Yet inwardly he felt a tinge of guilt. He was well aware that he had neglected the defense of other settlements in the Colony in order to preserve the security of Kingstown at all costs.

"*Aye sir! Lord knows our lads neva' stood a chance. Dey were outnumbad and outgunned by da wild negroes an' da French. Would've been a bwoody massacre if dey'd tried to hol' out much wonga.*"

The Governor grimaced visibly. His thin lips quivered uncontrollably as he spoke, almost as if he was talking more to himself than to his aide-de-camp. "*The devil take the hindmost![1] H-how could they have moved so swiftly? The treacherous French planters must have helped them. Blast those bloody traitors. I should've expelled them when I had the chance. It'll surely not be long before Kingstown is within their wretched clutches!*"

The Governor lapsed into silence as he paced back and forth restively, letting the news sink in. He wondered if he had

112

underestimated the wild negroes. Surely the French had assisted them in orchestrating this insidious assault on Chateaubelair. It defied belief that such savages were capable of pulling off such a coordinated military operation.

"*We must sound the alarm right away Lieutenant! The Militia and the Regiment at the Fort must be warned. The enemy attack could come at any moment!*"

"*Yes Gov'na. I'll make sure dey are awerted right away.*"

After a brief pause, Lieutenant George added sheepishly, "*Oh and one more thing sir. I.. er hate to be da beara of only bad news...*"

"*What's it now Lieutenant?*" snapped Governor Seton with mounting annoyance in his voice, as he glared at him with a fiery, almost threatening look.

"*On da windward coast several disturbing reports 've been tricklin' in from settlas and miwitiamen near Cawiaqua and Carapan. Apparently da wild negroes are cuttin' people to pieces. Choppin' off arms, hands an' wegs. Absowute barbarism Gov'na.*" Lieutenant George knitted his brows as his face unconsciously contorted in agony when he described the rabid brutality of the Black Caribs against the British and their partisans.

"*Those savages! We should've exterminated them ages ago.*"

"*Aye sir. Da devil knows it'd serve 'em bwoody cannibals right!*"[2]

113

Governor Seton dismissed his aide-de camp brusquely before stalking morosely back to his sleeping chambers. The tenor of his thoughts had become dark and loathsome as he grappled with the latest news. He reproached himself harshly for not previously taking the threat of the Black Caribs more seriously. Their rapid territorial gains had made it apparent that he had grossly misjudged their capabilities and that the tide of the war was turning precariously in their favor. Equally worrying were the rumors of their barbarity in subduing their enemies which would strike fear into even the stoutest hearts. This would make it harder to motivate the Militia to stand and fight in defense of Kingstown. The Governor was also wary that the Black Caribs might spread a radical message of emancipation that could sway the Colony's slave population to turn against the British at any moment, as the French had done when they retook Guadeloupe in the previous year.[3] He was convinced more than ever that he had to take drastic and decisive action soon, otherwise it would be too late to avert a disaster.

"*What was that all about James?*" inquired Josephine, momentarily upsetting the Governor's cascading train of thought.

"*Oh 'twas nothing to fret about my bonnie,*"[4] replied Governor Seton evasively.

"*It was about the war wasn't it? Those wretched wild negroes again? I always knew they could never be trusted. They should've been in chains like slaves. Working in the fields. That's*

114

what Africans are good for you know." As she spoke, Josephine self-consciously inspected the caramel tint of the skin on her bosom and arms trying in vain to mentally erase any trace of her mother's negro blood. She fancied herself as almost white. If it were not for her full lips, wide nose and thick, well-rounded hips, she was convinced that her African ancestry would barely be discernible to even the most scrutinous European eyes.

The Governor hardly paid attention to what Josephine was saying. His mind was preoccupied with plotting his next steps in the war. Without answering her question, he absentmindedly embraced her, pressing his lips affectionately against her forehead while inhaling her delicious aroma, before heading out to his office.

Remarkably, it would only be a few hours later that Governor Seton's spirits were lifted. The Royal Navy sloop, the HMS *Zebra* had anchored in Kingstown Bay, and unloaded forty men from the Forty-sixth Regiment of Foot along with a much needed consignment of arms and ammunition.[5] Thankfully Lieutenant General Vaughn in Martinique had not turned a deaf ear to the Governor's desperate appeal. Governor Seton hoped even more reinforcements from Barbados would soon follow. It was now clear that this was the best chance for the Colony's survival. The specter of defeat at the hands of savages was not something that he had the temerity to countenance.

CH16

~~~

An iridescent wine-red sunset stained the late afternoon sky as if the heavens too were hemorrhaging from all the bloodletting taking place in Hiroona. The colorful, winding wisps of burgundy, maroon and ruby-tinted clouds faded with the dying light, as darkness cast its shadowy cloak slowly over the island. Chief Chatoyé, sat together with his lieutenants, Joyette, Lalime and Citoyen Touraille, hunched over the sprawling mahogany dining table of a plantation great house plotting the leeward army's next move. On his orders, the advancing joint Garifuna and French force had halted at Chateaubelair to consolidate their rapid territorial gains and prepare for the coming final push towards Kingstown, a full day's march away.

Despite their campaign's resounding success till then, a peculiar, languid mood hung in the air. This was chiefly due to the French planters, who had failed to join their ranks en masse as had been initially anticipated. Many of them, despite having their property mostly left unmolested by Chatoyé's marauding army, were hedging their bets on the outcome of the war, and were reluctant to commit themselves fully against the British. This naturally put the French revolutionaries in an awkward position, making them eager to prove their compatriots' commitment to overthrow Britain's hegemony over the island.

"*We've got to take decisive action now General!*" urged Joyette," *The British threaten to regain strength with each passing day. We can't afford to sit here idly waiting for these French planters to join our cause! With or without them the war must go on!*" As he spoke these words in French, he forcefully thumped the mahogany table with his fist, punctuating every sentence with a resounding thud.

Regarding him with a sympathetic look in his eyes, Chief Chatoyé responded evenly, "*We must urgently find a way to rally them to our cause! Once our ranks are swelled, we'll make a more formidable force against the British in Kingstown.*"

"*There's no doubt the real fighting will begin when we reach the British bastion. So far it's been child's play. We'll surely need every man we can muster be they Frenchman, slave or otherwise,*" chimed in Lalime matter-of-factly, as he lustily eyed a half-drunken bottle of red wine standing on the table to the right of Joyette, who's drooping, bloodshot eyes betrayed his weariness from the previous night's ouïcou. Turning his attention towards Citoyen Touraille, seated to his left, Lalime enquired offhandedly, "*Pray, tell us brother why is it that your countrymen resist our cry for liberty?*"

The question racked Citoyen Touraille for a few moments before he could offer an answer. He prevaricated, "*Well, my dear*

117

Charaibes… I feel their hesitation is rooted in fear of the revolution. One hardly needs to look further than the tragedy happening in Haiti to apprehend their plight.[1] The revolution has spread like a wretched plague there. The negro slaves have risen up against the planters and formed an army which has visited utter ruin upon them these past years." He vigorously stroked the stubble on his chin as he spoke, enjoying the feel of the rough, unshaven hair rubbing against the back of his hand. Citoyen Touraille did this reflexively whenever he had a captive audience.

"*And the good lord knows we mustn't bungle like we did in Guadeloupe last year. Oh mon Dieu what a disastre that was!*"

Pausing for dramatic effect, Citoyen Touraille waited for the chiefs to prod him further on this subject, before continuing his discourse.

"*What do you mean?*" enquired Joyette fixing his gaze intently on Citoyen Touraille, who was seated across from him, causing him to briefly lose his train of thought.

"*Er…what I mean to say is that we mustn't free the slaves. Were that to happen then the French planters 'll surely turn against our cause. Just like in Guadeloupe when Governor Hugues arrived to retake it for France.[2] Sacrebleu! It was a catastrophe!*" Citoyen Touraille's face adopted an exaggerated expression of horror as these last words left his lips.

While he waited for his message to seep in, he searched the faces of Lalime, Joyette and Chief Chatoyé for a sign of

118

affirmation. Instead, he perceived a look of consternation in their eyes.

"*We have already many freed slaves fighting alongside us. Surely we can't deny them their freedom once they've already tasted it. That'd be worse than ripping a nursing baby from its mother's breast!*" rejoined Joyette, who had suddenly awoken from his seeming stupor.

"'*Tis true what you say Citoyen Joyette. For now, we profit greatly in destroying the British by freeing their slaves. Yet we must be mindful not to declare that slavery is abolished on the island. This is the only way we can be assured of the support of the French planters*," warned Citoyen Touraille.

"*Yet we've made no such proclamation, nor intend to,*" countered Lalime hoarsely, still thirsting for a swig of wine.

"*Your countrymen's fears are unfounded. Perhaps the root of their disaffection lies elsewhere? Surely they're not afraid to fight? Otherwise, such cowardice deserves to be rewarded with fire and sword!*" scoffed Lalime, contemptuously.

To this Citoyen Touraille could offer no reply beyond a defiant scowl that conveyed his displeasure at Lalime's insinuation.

Sensing a need to diffuse the tension in the room, Chief Chatoyé then stepped in to close the discussion. Studying the men carefully, he addressed them, "*I've heard enough brothers. As commander of this revolutionary army, it's now clear to me what*

119

we have to do. We must appeal to the planter's patriotic duty as Frenchmen. This will surely compel them to join our cause. If that fails then we shall reluctantly be forced to treat them as enemies and they'll face the same fate as the cursed British!" No sooner had these words left his lips, than Chief Chatoyé had grabbed the cutlass resting by his side and slammed it forcefully against one of the wooden side boards near the dining table as if to release the revolutionary fervor burning within him.[3]

With alacrity Chief Chatoyé set about drafting a declaration in French using a quill and ink retrieved from the former plantation owner's chambers.[4] When he was finished, by the dim light of a tallow candle, he read it aloud to his lieutenants:

Chateaubelair, 12th March and the first of our freedom Declaration:

Who is the Frenchman who will not join his brothers at a moment when the cry of liberty is heard by them? Let us then unite, citizens and brothers, around the flag which flies in the island and let us hasten to cooperate in the great work already so gloriously begun. But if any timid men should still exist, should any Frenchman be held back through fear, we do hereby declare to them in the name of the law that those who are not mustered with us within the day will be regarded as traitors to the country and treated as enemies. We swear to them that fire and the sword will be used against

them, that we will burn their goods and that we will slit the throats
of their wives and children to wipe out their race.

Ordinary mark † of Joseph Chatoyé

General

His words found a vivid response among the men. Even Citoyen Touraille, who was wary of undermining French strategic interests on the island consented with little fuss to the fiery wording. The following morning Chatoyé's declaration was read out loud to a gathering of French planters in the central square of Chateaubelair. By noon the leeward army had mobilized to continue its drive south to rendezvous with Duvallé's army. Chatoyé's skillful leadership had succeeded in rallying the French planters, along with their slaves.

In their hasty departure the rearguard of the leeward army took three Englishmen, who had been hiding out in a rum cellar on a plantation in Chateaubelair, prisoner. Their lives were spared, at least momentarily, by the imperatives of the war. Chained at the neck like slaves in a work gang, they unceremoniously joined the southward march of Chatoyé's forces towards Kingstown.

Meanwhile, on the windward side of the island Duvallé's men had continued their relentless onslaught against the British and had captured Calliaqua, just two and a half miles from Kingstown. The small pockets of resistance they faced along the way, had been effortlessly overcome, leaving his forces largely intact. By mid-morning they reached the summit of Dorsetshire Hill, which had a commanding view of the capital. Duvallé wasted no time in lowering the British flag and raising the French Tricolor. With the French flag now flying above Kingstown, within clear view of Fort Charlotte, the war was now decidedly on Governor Seton's doorsill. Direct confrontation with the British forces garrisoned in the capital was henceforth inevitable. It would undoubtedly be a violent clash to decide the fate of Hiroona.

122

PART III: Vae Victis

As one who long hath fled with panting breath
Before his foe, bleeding and near to fall,
I turn and set my back against the wall,
And look thee in the face, triumphant Death,
I call for aid, and no one answereth;
I am alone with thee, who conquerest all;
Yet me thy threatening form doth not appall,
For thou art but a phantom and a wraith.
Wounded and weak, sword broken at the hilt,
With armor shattered, and without a shield,
I stand unmoved; do with me what thou wilt;
I can resist no more, but will not yield.
This is no tournament where cowards tilt;
The vanquished here is victor of the field.

(Henry Wadsworth Longfellow – excerpted from Victor and
Vanquished, published in 1882 in the anthology In the Harbor)

CH17

~~~

Warramou woke up in the pitch blackness of the middle of the night, drenched in a cold sweat, with his body wracked by shudders. For some reason, which was impossible for him to fathom, Pa Louen had appeared vividly in his dreams. Warramou saw himself as a young boy, not long weaned from his mother's breast,[1] sitting on his grandfather's lap attentively listening to him tell a story. Yet there was something bizarre about his grandfather this time. His voice possessed a peculiar tinny quality. In fact, Warramou could not make out Pa Louen's words since they were so faint. However, he could see from the grave language of his body that his grandfather was trying to warn him about something.

Frustrated by his inability to comprehend Pa Louen, young Warramou had craned his neck upwards until he could peer directly into his grandfather's eyes. As their eyes locked, Warramou noticed that Pa Louen's face had lost its familiar wizened, leathery appearance. Instead, he looked like a young man, not much older than Warramou's present age, with his unmistakably Carib features, high cheekbones and flat forehead, glaringly visible. As he studied him further, Warramou observed that Pa Louen's brows were furrowed and his eyes were narrowed, giving him a bleak visage, that he had never seen before.

All of sudden Pa Louen's face became suffused with a shaft of brilliant sunlight. Simultaneously his voice became clearer to Warramou, who could finally make out the words emanating from Pa Louen's lips.

"Beware my son of not heeding destiny's call. Rise up and embrace your warrior's fate. Lead our people to vanquish their enemy in this righteous war. We, offspring of the Ocean God, must not rest till the last drop of enemy blood has been spilled to quench Qualeva's thirst. For His wrath knows no bounds."

With his solemn exhortation delivered Pa Louen turned away, casting his gaze towards an obscure point in the distance, while clenching his fists and slowly muttering under his breath, *"Ana, cariná rote! Aucion paparoto mantoro itoto manto! Only we are people! There are no cowards here, nobody gives up, this land is ours!"*[2]

Pa Louen then fell silent as he vanished into thin air before young Warramou's eyes. It was then that Warramou had awoken and found himself shivering and soaked in cold sweat.

Warramou lay awake for several minutes pondering the meaning of this cryptic dream, which he was certain presaged an ominous turn in the ongoing war. What bewildered him most of all were Pa Louen's mysterious words about embracing his fate to lead their people. Surely this made no sense. Chief Chatoyé and his brother, Chief Duvallé, the most admired and experienced Garifuna warriors, were already spearheading the Garifuna war

126

effort with great success. Perhaps this was a sign that the war was about to go down a more violent and deadly path. One that was destined to result in a desperate fight to the death with the British for control of Hiroona. Peaceful coexistence would never again be possible.

Rattled by his dream and its baleful implications, Warramou found himself unable to doze off again. To clear his head, he decided to take a stroll around the perimeter of the summit of Dorsetshire Hill. When he reached the outermost fortified wall, on the leeward side of the hill, overlooking Kingstown, he paused to observe the lights shimmering eerily from Fort Charlotte. He studied the scene assiduously for a moment as if it was on the verge of revealing a divine secret to him, yet it remained just beyond his grasp. In the half-light of the pre-dawn Warramou did, however, discover that he was not alone. He had in fact already sensed it, before confirming it with his eyes, as they adjusted to the dimness. Seated near the ledge, thirty odd paces away from where he was standing there was another Garifuna warrior. From the delicate shape of the silhouette, he quickly deduced that it was a female. Her gaze too was intently fixed in the direction of Kingstown, yet he knew intuitively that she was aware of his presence.

Warramou contemplated walking away quietly, but thought better of it and instead approached the silhouetted stranger, with whom he felt a mysterious connection. When he

127

reached within a few paces he was certain that he recognized her slender sinewy frame. It was Nanette. He had not seen her since the night that the war had begun five days prior.

Addressing Nanette in French, Warramou began, *"Nan, is that you? Where've you been hiding all this time?"*

Nanette turned her head towards Warramou and greeted him warmly with her eyes. She seemed unsurprised to see him, but responded to his greeting in a measured tone, to conceal her avid excitement. *"I's wonderin' when I's go see yo 'gain Mistuh Warramou. Taught yo forget 'bout me."*

"That's impossible Nan. My body still bears the scars of your handiwork from our fight. You have definitely left a lasting impression on me," came Warramou's reply as his voice dissolved infectiously into laughter.

Nanette smiled in response and then playfully added, *"Yo lucky I's gone easy on yo dat time Mistuh Warramou. Don' tink dat I forget de horruble taase of yo boutou!"*

Warramou chuckled softly as he recalled his cheeky taunts during their feisty clash. As he reflected on that moment, his mind unconsciously drifted to the looming, pivotal battle that would be fought for Kingstown. He was grateful that Nan was no longer an enemy combatant, and would instead fight alongside him to push the British out of Hiroona.

Giving voice to these thoughts Warramou exclaimed excitedly, *"Can you believe it Nan? Soon we're going to attack*
128

Kingstown and we'll finish driving the wretched British out of Hiroona." While making a sweeping gesture towards Fort Charlotte, he added, *"We'll control all the land you see before you! Even that fort over yonder."*

"Yeh. We ah go wipe dem out and free up all de slaves in Hiroona too! Finally we go be rid uh dem! And I go see Ma en Babs 'gain!"

These last words gushed emphatically out of Nanette's mouth, like a fire spreading through dry brush. This was due to the fact that her mother and younger sister, Babette, were still enslaved on a plantation elsewhere on the island. She had not seen or heard from them in several years and desperately longed to be reunited with them. Nanette had in fact kept these thoughts to herself all this time and had never previously shared them with anyone. Yet Warramou had somehow pierced her tough outer shell and she found herself pouring her heart out to him.

"I-I ain't seen Ma 'n muh baby sis, Babs, in ova four years. Since de time wen Massa Dubois in Barrouallie sol' me off to Mad'me La Croix fuh a dept he been owed. Is been so hard widout dem 'round. Yo don' know Mistuh Warramou. Somes I feels I jus caan go on no more! I jus' caan!" As Nanette spoke these words tears welled up in her eyes and she began to sob uncontrollably. Her body was soon consumed in violent convulsions as she struggled in vain to master her emotions. Not wanting Warramou to see that she had lost control, she deliberately turned her face

129

away from him. Warramou in turn reacted by instinctively drawing himself closer to her and placing the palm of his left hand affectionately on Nanette's right shoulder while whispering in her ear soothingly, *"I'm sorry Nan. I can hardly imagine how hard it has been for you. I promise you a new dawn of freedom will begin in Hiroona after we expel the British!"*

As he said this, Pa Louen's last words came to him and he added with verve, *"Ana, cariná rote! Aucion paparoto mantoro itoto manto! Only we are people! There are no cowards here, nobody gives up, this land is ours!"*

Finding comfort in these words, Nanette's sobbing slowly subsided until silence descended upon them and they were both left alone with their thoughts. The sun's rays were just beginning to peer over the horizon when they parted ways. It was an unremarkable start to what would be the most pivotal day in the war.

CH18

~~~

Governor Seton flew into a rage at the sight of the blue, white and red, French Tricolor flying from the flagstaff on the summit of Dorsetshire Hill. The veins in his forehead throbbed visibly as blood rushed to his head flushing his normally pale, gaunt cheeks cherry red. He was like a man possessed by fever. His worst nightmare seemed to be coming true right before his eyes. The imperial British presence was now confined to an inconsiderable strip of territory around Kingstown, sandwiched between the vast Caribbean Sea and the hostile hinterland of St. Vincent. Equally disturbing, was his crumbling esteem as a leader, which was on the verge of collapsing under the weight of the mounting losses. Each day seemed to bring another setback, highlighting his ineptitude in managing this morass that was slowly spiraling out of control.

For a moment, in a fit of despair, the Governor pictured his sordid demise at the hands of the wild negroes. The thought wrenched the breath from him, as his mood grew blacker and blacker. He could not deign to countenance surrendering the colony to such savages. Above all else, he was certain of one thing. The fate of Governor Home in Grenada would never befall him. He refused to ever let that happen. He would muster the

131

courage to take his own life rather than capitulate and face the barbaric vengeance of heathens.

These macabre thoughts seething in Governor Seton's head were displaced by the arrival of Captain Lancelot Skynner, commander of the HMS *Zebra* and his second in command, Lieutenant Norborne Thompson.[1] Both men were career Royal Navy men who, in contrast to the Governor's state of abysmal despondency, carried themselves with a relaxed ease and calm confidence. However, it was there that the similarity between the two men ended.

Captain Skynner, for his part was stouter and by the look of his slightly greying, woolly mutton chops,[2] was at least a decade older than Lieutenant Thompson. He was thickset, with a corpulent face and a stern, implacable aspect. He was well known for his volatile, tinderbox temper, which could flare up unpredictably, especially after he had been drinking. It had in fact cost him a promotion in the Royal Navy on at least two occasions in the past.

Lieutenant Thompson by contrast was clean-shaven, with a medium build and a comely face, dotted with freckles. He was easily distinguished by his unruly mop of red hair, which he wore cropped short in a Roman fashion à la Brutus,[3] and by his bright, beady, blue eyes, which danced around whenever he became excited.

"Good morrow Governor. We 'ope we ain't intrudin' upon your 'xcellency. Captain Skynner sir, Lancelot Skynner at your

132

service and dis is my second in comman', Lieutenant Norborne Thompson," offered Captain Skynner casually, as he extended his hand blithely.

"Good morrow gentlemen. I've been expecting your arrival most eagerly," replied the Governor while firmly shaking each of their hands, in turn. The slight tremor in his voice as he spoke, offered the only discernible hint of his abject frame of mind.

"'pologies for da delay sir. We wuz detained at da 'arbor with a wee concern of one of da crew. Not to worry tho'. We smooved it all out. E'erything's as right as my leg now."[4] The Captain grinned an almost toothless smile while he spoke these words and let out a deep barrel-chested laugh, which almost succeeded in diffusing the awkward tension brewing in the room.

Despite the Governor's best efforts Captain Skynner could see plainly through the Governor's charade, smelling the fear consuming him like the stench of rotting codfish at the bottom of a barrel. Slightly put off by the sight of such a powerful man in a fragile state, the Captain hesitantly enquired, *"So how may we be...Ahem... at your 'xcellency's disposal?"*

"I suppose, gentlemen, you've already been briefed on the dire situation we're in. This diabolical war is presently not unfolding in the Crown's favor. The enemy is at our threshold, having taken up an offensive position on Dorsetshire Hill, less than two miles away from us. I fear an attack is imminent." The Governor paused briefly to let the urgency of his words hit home before continuing.

Casting an expectant gaze towards the two men, which conveyed the unshakable faith that he was desperately placing in them to save the Colony, he went on, *"Our defenses may not be able to withstand the enemy onslaught. We've just this morning received a report from a Militia unit stationed near Sion Hill, that they've dismantled the fort at Stubbs Bay and are dragging two canons towards their position on the summit of Dorsetshire Hill.[5] Were they to succeed in these efforts this would spell certain disaster for us. We must take vigorous measures before it's too late. I-I refuse to cower helplessly in this fort..."*

Captain Skynner cut him off exuberantly with his clamorous voice, *"Don't worry milord. We'll sort dis mess out. Just like we did in Mart'nique las' year. We routed 'em stinking frog-eaters.[6] Absolutely thrashed 'em, didn't we Lieutenant?"*

As Captain Skynner spoke these words, Lieutenant Thompson's beady, blue eyes began to shine radiantly indicating that he was keen to speak, but he remained silent.

"Brilliant! That's exactly what I was counting on Captain. Although I should warn you, the French presently are not the chief concern. It's their cronies, the wretched wild negroes, that are the main cause of the present havoc," offered the Governor. The force in his voice had returned, indicating that he was beginning to pull himself together.

134

"*Have no fear your 'xcellency. We're agog for a good fight! Isn't dat right Lieutenant?*" roared Captain Skynner, with a wink at his second in command.

"*Yes sir. Our lads are hungry for battle. It doesn't matter if we're up against the French, wild negroes or Barbary pirates. We'll take 'em on all the same sir!*" boasted Lieutenant Thompson expansively.

Measuring the men gravely with his gaze, the Governor urged them to channel their bravado into drawing up a plan for a British counterattack. He summoned Lieutenant George to bring forth a map of Dorsetshire Hill and the surrounding terrain, which he spread out onto his small, waxed-honey-colored mahogany, kneehole desk. Being keenly aware that a French military garrison had been stationed there during the last occupation of the island just over a decade prior, he also requested Lieutenant George to retrieve the blueprint of the extensive military installations and fortifications on the hills' summit from the colonial archives.[7]

Captain Skynner and Lieutenant Thompson pored over the sheafs of papers eagerly. They exchanged glances and periodic grunts of satisfaction and dismay whenever they spotted an interesting feature that might be advantageous or detrimental in combat.

"*The enemy's position seems quite formidable your 'xcellency. They've secured high ground very difficult of access. It gives dem a commanding position above da town and harbor of*

135

Kingstown, and direct line o' sight to Fort Charlotte. Canons mounted on dis ridge would be most devastating to our cause!" observed Captain Skynner candidly. He was never one to shy away from sharing his thoughts out loud.

"Indeed Captain. It would seem on the surface nigh impossible to overtake the enemy's position." He paused to clear his throat before continuing, "Yet all is not lost. The terrain surrounding the hill seems to be heavily wooded, with steep winding paths, well hidden from view. This could perhaps provide us the necessary cover to carry out an attack," ventured Lieutenant Thompson constructively.

"And what is da best estimate of da enemy strength Governor?" enquired the Captain, without even looking up from studying the map.

"At present, we believe somewhere in the region of three to four hundred men including the French revolutionary troops," offered the Governor feebly, betraying the fact that he himself was doubtful of the veracity of the numbers he was sharing.

"Hmmm. That's a formidable force. Rationally speaking, a conventional attack is out of the question Governor. Certainly not in broad daylight. That'd be bloody madness. With three score men we'll be cut to pieces!" noted Lieutenant Thompson with brutal honesty.

"Aye, da situation seems to call for a more discrete approach. We must neutralize da advantage of deer s'perior

136

numbers," urged Captain Skynner, who by now was beginning to conjure up a plan in his head.

"If we attack unda cover of darkness, when da enemy is off deer guard, we'd 'ave ample time to spike deer canons befo' dey can train 'em on Kingstown." As he continued the tone of his voice became more thundering, confirming his growing conviction in the plan being hatched.

"That'd perhaps allow us to stall 'em long enough for reinforcements to arrive from Martinique and Barbados. Then we can turn the tide of this war in our favor," added Lieutenant Thompson, with a twinkle in his beady blue eyes.

Governor Seton and Captain Skynner nodded their heads in agreement.

"Aye Captain. This reminds me of the operation we conducted in Martinique last March when we stormed Fort Saint Louis. Caught those Frog-eaters off guard. We put ev'ry one of 'em to the bayonet and turned the battle into a route for Admiral Jervis!"[8] blustered Lieutenant Thompson fervently, his eyes dancing ecstatically, as he recounted this anecdote.

"Aye, dat was indeed a brilliant raid. For da loss of jus' one man and four wounded if mem'ry serves me right," added Captain Skynner gleefully thumping the Governor's kneehole desk with his fist as he spoke.

Clasping both men warmly on their shoulders, the Governor, buoyed by their confidence, was exuberant:

137

"*Bravo Gentlemen. Let's put this plan into action. All necessary resources of the Colony are at your disposal. The Crown is much obliged for your honorable service, in her hour of great need!*"

At that moment, Lieutenant George burst into the room brimming with excitement.

"*Gov'na. I've received some news that should lift thy spirits!*"

Without waiting for a reaction from Governor Seton, he blurted out, "*The HMS Roebuck has just been spotted offshore. She'll make landfall by early afternoon.*"

"*Brilliant! This is the answer to our prayers,*" replied Governor Seton, his voice nakedly exuding the growing sense of relief that was overtaking him. He hoped that this desperate gamble to save the Colony would pay off. The consequences of failure were unconscionable.

CH19

~~~

When Chatoyé's army reached Dorsetshire Hill, the mood in Duvallé's camp was restless, like the turbid morning sky overhead. The men were tired. Not out of weariness from fighting or marching through the night. They were tired of waiting and anticipating the next battle. Of preparing for combat and facing an elusive enemy, that seemed to be avoiding head-on confrontation. The men wanted more than anything to see action and eagerly thirsted for British blood. Their bloodlust was almost driving them to madness as they struggled to find useful ways to expend their pent up reservoirs of frustration. Brawling and bickering impetuously about matters quickly forgotten, were the only meagre outlets at their disposal.

Perceiving the tension lurking in the air, Chatoyé quickly sought to diffuse it. He knew only too well that emotional torrents like this could easily boil over, and do more harm than good to their cause if left undissipated. He ordered the three British prisoners, captured by the rearguard near Chateaubelair, during his leeward army's hasty departure, to be brought out before him. He did this purposefully in full view of the throng of Garifuna warriors, French planters, French revolutionaries and slaves milling restively around the summit of the hill.

One by one each shirtless prisoner was led out, shackled at the hands and feet like slaves on the auction block. As their names were solemnly called out, "*Duncan Cruikshank. Peter Cruikshank. William Grant,*" they hung their heads low, with their sunken, defeated-looking eyes fixed on the ground in shame.[1] Not daring to look up at each other for strength, nor at Chatoyé for compassion, they stood languidly under the protruding gaze of the scores of hostile, bloodthirsty eyes surrounding them, awaiting their fate.

Addressing the crowd of onlookers, Chatoyé began vociferously, "*My brothers, you have heeded our cry of liberty that rings out across this land, it is time for us to enter a new, decisive phase of this war. We shall not rest till the last vestiges of the British are extirpated from Hiroona with fire and sword.*" This elicited a thunderous round of cheers and howls, briefly drowning out the paramount Chief's voice as he continued his bitter invective.

Turning his attention to the British prisoners, he slowly withdrew his rapier from its sheath at his side. The very same sword gifted him by Citoyen Touraille on behalf of Governor Hugues, prior to the start of the war. Brandishing it, Chatoyé proclaimed, "*From this day forth no Englishman's life shall be spared our wrath. We shall make them suffer for coveting our land, seeking to deprive us of our liberty and for trying to destroy our noble way of life. Our rage against their inhumanity and injustice*
140

will not relent until the rivers of Hiroona turn red with their blood. We will burn their goods, slit the throats of their wives and children, until we wipe them out from the face of this land."

As he spoke these words, amid a deluge of sonorous whooping and hollering, he lunged towards the first prisoner, who had been standing a few paces away, and struck him violently across the neck with his saber, severing his jugular vein with one slash. As he continued excoriating the British, with each indictment he delivered, blow after blow rained down upon the prisoner until his entrails leaked out before him and he collapsed on the ground mortally wounded. Chatoyé then moved onto the second prisoner, Peter Cruikshank, who cowered in fear at the bloodied sight of his fallen brother. Under a relentless flurry of slashes Chatoyé cut him to pieces until he too crumpled in a pool of burgundy-colored blood at Chatoyé's feet. Then it was the turn of William Grant, who cried out to the Lord for mercy as he was gruesomely chopped to death where he stood.[2]

As each Englishmen met his fate, an ecstatic cacophony of jeers and epithets filled the air, at one point becoming so voluble that they muted the petrified screams issuing from the men's mouths as they breathed their last. Once the final corpse fell unceremoniously to the ground, Chatoyé raised his bloodstained rapier in triumph while bellowing the war cry, *"Ana, cariná rote. Aucion paparoto mantoro itoto manto! Only we are people! There are no cowards here, nobody gives up, this land is ours!"* This

141

electrified the crowd, which responded by zealously echoing the war cry for several minutes after. This was the crescendo that Chatoyé had sought to achieve.

With the crowd's lust for blood momentarily satiated, and Chief Chatoyé's fit of rage past, he wiped the blade of his sword clean with his loincloth before calmly returning it to the sheath at his side. He then abruptly strode off towards Duvallé's headquarters in the main barracks, to begin planning the assault on Kingstown. There he found his brother, and his lieutenants, Massoteau, Dufond, and Warramou embroiled in a heated discussion.

"We should've already driven the British into the sea and be roaming the streets of Kingstown by now. We must attack tonight or all will be lost! One more day of idle hesitation will be our ruin!" growled Dufond fiercely, drawing venom from the seething pain shooting through his wounded hip.

"That'd be sheer madness, brother. Without French support we'll be decimated by the British canons," retorted Massoteau defiantly.

"Brother Dufond is right. We must strike now while the iron is hot. Let's take the fight to the enemy's threshold," urged Warramou excitedly. He was clearly rearing to fight.

"We must find the right moment to attack. I'm confident it will present itself soon," cautioned Duvallé, who was keen to see the attack plan that he had conceived succeed.

Chief Chatoyé listened patiently for a few moments, until a brief lull in the debate presented an opportunity for him to interject. He greeted the men warmly.

"Buiti binafi. Good morning, brothers."

"Buiti binafi. Good morning, brother Chatoyé. You've made it at last! How'd it go on the leeward coast?" enquired Duvallé eagerly. His eyes beaming with a boyish delight as he embraced his brother warmly with a firm slap on his shoulder.

"There isn't much to report. We captured Chateaubelair, Troumaca, Barrouallie and Layou with little resistance. Then we marched through the night to reach here as soon as possible. Everything's gone according to plan so far. Even the French settlers have been convinced to join our cause," offered Chief Chatoyé in a dispassionate, matter-of-fact tone.

Chief Chatoyé's haste in reaching Dorsetshire Hill, the designated rendezvous point with Duvallé's windward army, was due in no small part to his realization that the weakened position of the British could easily be reversed at a moment's notice by the arrival of reinforcements. Time was of the essence in order for Duvallé's plan to succeed. At the same time, Chief Chatoyé, like Massoteau, was wary of initiating a direct assault on Kingstown without French commitment on the ground and from the sea. The support of Governor Hugues' invading force from Guadeloupe was an essential ingredient for success. Yet the French troops had not yet materialized despite repeated assurances from Citoyen

143

Touraille that they were underway. Attacking too soon or too late could prove to be fatal to their cause.

This dilemma was weighing heavily on Chatoyé's mind as he asked Duvallé for a report on his army, *"And how'd you fare on the windward coast?"*

"We arrived here yesterday after destroying everything crossing our path, with few losses and a handful of wounded. The men are now busy dragging a twelve-pounder and a four-pounder into position. Once we mount these canons, I expect we'll be ready to launch the attack on Kingstown by dawn tomorrow," Duvallé got this report out proudly, hardly pausing to take a breath. He was keen to show his brother that the windward army had performed to expectation.

"Excellent. And what is the latest information on the enemy's disposition in Kingstown?"

"They have withdrawn to Fort Charlotte. According to our lookouts on the coast they've recently received some reinforcements and munitions from Jouanacaeira.[3] A sloop docked yesterday in the harbor and a corvette was spotted on the horizon this morning," reported Duvallé with a concerned look in his eyes.

"Hmmmph. It is unsurprising that the British refuse to stay idle. Our window of opportunity to strike may be closing soon."

Chatoyé paused for a moment to gather his thoughts, before continuing, *"And our French allies haven't arrived yet from*

Karukera? Without their support I'm afraid that taking Kingstown 'll not be easy."

Looking his brother directly in the eye, Duvallé rejoined rashly, *"I'm not sure brother. Perhaps it's folly to wait on the French. We clearly have the upper hand at the moment, and are now poised to deliver a decisive blow against the British. We must act swiftly before the tide of the war turns against us."*

"What you speak is truth, brother. The battle for Kingstown will surely be a bloody one. Our advantage lies in fighting from the bush not in the open as Europeans favor. The French know well how to wage war in this way. It is best we seek the boyez's guidance so that the will of the Gods can guide us in this matter. Qualeva's thirst for blood will surely not be quenched until we drive the last Englishman out of Yurumein."

The fate of Hiroona was now out of their hands. It was up to the gods to divine the hour of their attack. Till then they would bide their time like a snake lurking in the grass waiting to pounce on its prey and release its deadly venom.

CH20

~~~

Shortly after midnight, a band of forty militiamen and dragoons, along with a detachment from the Forty-sixth Regiment of Foot, set out in single file along the steep, winding slopes of Dorsetshire Hill in regularity and silence.[1] Governor Seton had issued the final order to attack the enemy's position only moments prior. He dared not hesitate any longer out of fear that Kingstown would be destroyed if the Black Caribs and their French allies were allowed to possess this strategic location for another day. It would only be a matter of time before they would train their captured canons on the town, wreaking havoc.

As the intrepid British force furtively ascended towards the summit, under the faint glimmer of a waning moon, they could already hear the low murmuring sounds of their unsuspecting foes growing louder and louder by the minute. At a fork in the pathway, still some ways from the top, as planned, the detachment from the Forty-sixth, split off and headed towards the south side of the ridge.[2] Under the able command of Captain Dugald Campbell of the HMS *Roebuck*, a distinguished veteran of military campaigns in Guadeloupe and Martinique. Their role would be to divert the enemy's attention from the main body of the attack. The remaining core of the force, led by Captain Lancelot Skynner, with support from Lieutenant Norborne Thompson continued their slow climb along the leeward slope of the hill, cloaked in near pitch blackness, amid bushes and broken ground.

Among the ranks of the militiamen supporting Captain Skynner's dragoons, was Captain Alexander Leith. He had been among the first of his peers to volunteer for this daredevil mission. However, his initial exuberance was slowly giving way to a more sobering realization. The adrenaline diffusing through his veins was making the hair on the back of his neck stand on end. With each advancing step he could feel the knots in his stomach tightening, and his heart pumping harder in his chest. It's insistent pounding was deafening, almost overpowering his other senses, which were on high alert. A singular thought dominated his mind in that moment. Survival. He wanted to make it out of this operation alive. Till then he had never bestowed significance on what it would feel like to risk his life in combat. He had always boyishly glamorized combat in his head, ignoring the perils of battle in favor of its romantic allure of adventure and conquest. Yet the full gravity of this oversight finally struck him in this incipient moment of apprehension as he wended his way towards an uncertain destiny on the summit of Dorsetshire Hill.

After a sharp bend in the trail, Alexander and the main force found themselves within eighty yards of the main enemy post. At that point, long shafts of pale light emanating from the fires lit by the Black Carib and French fighters, camped on the hill's crest, came into view. A hush came over the men as they endeavored to quickly attain the summit undetected. In their haste to achieve their objective, one of the dragoons in the vanguard tripped and stepped on a fallen branch, causing a loud snapping noise to echo through the hillside. Immediately, they were challenged by a sentry in French.[3]

"*Who goes there?*"

When no response was forthcoming, the guard opened fire, while raising the alarm. The shot whizzed harmlessly into the darkness overhead as the British troops surged towards the embankment. With the element of surprise lost, they quickly abandoned stealth in favor of expediency. Alexander could hear loud war cries of "*Buaidh no bàs! Victory or death!*" ahead of him as his compatriots charged forth, engaging their foes with a relentless volley of fire. The intensity of the fusillade was confirmed by the persistent ringing in his ears. The only reprieve from this thunderous tumult came from its intermittent punctuation by the rhythmic thrusting of ramrods, as musket barrels were hastily cleaned and reloaded with gunpowder and shot for the next wave of firing.

Alexander bit down on his lip and then ran as hard as he could towards the faint light, some twenty yards ahead. Scrambling the last few steps, before clamoring up the embankment. No longer sheltered by the dense, shadowy, undergrowth, he instantly felt exposed on the expansive summit.
148

Instinctively, he crouched down close to the ground making himself small to avoid the gale of musket shot flying overhead in all directions. He proceeded by crawling slowly forward on his belly towards the newly established British foothold on the leeward side of the summit near the flagstaff.

Undismayed by the surprise attack, the Garifuna and their French allies responded quickly by returning a smart fire of musketry on the British troops as they breached the summit. Not long after, the first of several waves of fighters came hurtling fearlessly towards the British lines. They were mowed down by the unremitting barrage of musket fire laid by the veteran dragoons, closely supported by the militiamen. Those among the Garifuna and French fighters who were unscathed, hastily withdrew out of range of the deadly hail of lead raining down upon them. This permitted the British to advance further and firmly establish their frontline on the hill's crest.

Quickly recognizing that the enemy was on the backfoot, Captain Skynner pressed home their advantage. Screaming at the top of his lungs, he gave the command for his men to close ranks and fix bayonets. This order passed down the line and was obeyed with alacrity by the militiamen and dragoons alike, who were relishing the chance for shock action against an enemy that had been softened by musket fire. They were ready to put to the knife anything and anyone that made resistance as they cleared the hill.

In the meantime, Captain Campbell's detachment had scaled the second embankment unnoticed. Their entry point, being on the far side of the hill, towards the south, had afforded them easy access to the enemy artillery, less than fifty yards away. They wasted no time in capturing and disabling the two cannons, by driving barbed steel rods into the touchholes and then blowing off their trunnions with gunpowder.[4] All the while they faced little resistance from their adversaries, who were caught off-guard by the second front of the attack. Amid the ensuing mayhem, several Black Carib and French fighters haplessly found themselves in the crosshairs of a burst of musket fire as they ran frantically away from the fierce firefight taking place on the leeward side of the hill.

As the battle wore on, Alexander, immersed himself in the thick of combat, shoulder-to-shoulder with his comrades. The swelling, noxious haze of gunpowder smoke enveloping the summit of the hill obscured the already murky conditions on the battlefield. Barely able to see more than a few paces in front of him, Alexander's eyes watered and his throat burned, from the sulfuric fumes. Yet he succeeded in repeatedly discharging his musket at the enemy forces fleeing in disarray in all directions. Lacking a bayonet, instead he used his sword to menace enemy combatants as the British line surged forth. Alexander was certain that he had singlehandedly killed at least two fighters, and wounded at least half a dozen others, if not more. It was hard to be sure in the weak half-light, yet he estimated that the battlefield was littered with at least two dozen bodies. Already his head was reeling from the adrenaline of his first live fire engagement of the war, notwithstanding the early morning raid on the Black Carib camp from six days prior. That operation hardly counted anymore since there hadn't been a firefight and no one had been killed. Henceforth one thing was certain. Alexander's taste for blood had been awakened.

However, the Black Caribs and their French allies were far from defeated. They were quickly regrouping and preparing to mount a spirited counterattack.

CH21

~~~

Warramou had been in a deep slumber when the first shots rang out. Initially unaware that an attack was underway, he had hardly stirred from the cozy nook behind the main barracks, which had become his preferred resting place. Being well accustomed to the restlessness of his fellow fighters in the camp, he had merely rolled over in his sleep in response to the fracas. Yet moments later when it became clear that the gunfire was persistent and accompanied by frenetic yelling, Warramou reluctantly stirred from his sleep to investigate what was happening. Out of sheer force of habit he reached for his boutou, bow and quiver of poison-tipped arrows, that had been lying nearby, and made his way along the back side of the barracks towards the sound of the gunfire.

Despite the dimness of the night, Warramou knew his way around the warren of structures on the summit of Dorsetshire Hill, having committed their layout to memory during the many hours he had spent traipsing around the fortifications on the previous night. He headed off in a leeward direction, having quickly perceived that the firing was coming from the side of the ridge nearest Kingstown. Turning a corner to the left and then making a sharp right at the armory, he emerged not long after at a vantage point, concealed behind a small bush, that offered him a glimpse of the source of the nocturnal disturbance that had awakened him.

To his right, despite the burgeoning haze of gunpowder smoke hovering over the summit, he could make out several bright orange and yellow-hued flashes of musket-fire, not far from the flagstaff, illuminating the darkness periodically like fireflies dancing in a stormy night sky. It was clear from the aim and ferocity of this fusillade that the British were attacking from this position. To his left he saw sporadic flickers of yellow and orange light indicating that his fellow Garifuna warriors and their French allies were beginning to mount resistance. Yet, as far as he could gauge, the counteroffensive seemed uncoordinated and ineffective. It was clearly insufficient to dislodge the British frontline, which was firmly established on the summit of the hill.

As Warramou looked on in dismay, he heard a succession of loud explosions coming from the southern side of the ridge. Unbeknownst to him Captain Campbell's men had at that instant succeeded in disabling the two cannons that had been painstakingly dragged for the past two days into position from the dismantled fort at Stubbs Bay. For a moment, Warramou contemplated rushing to the other side of the hill to investigate what was happening there. Yet he quickly changed his mind when he noticed with some alarm that the musket fire was beginning to encroach on the buildings close to his position. His concern was further heightened by the murderous, bloodcurdling shouts of the

153

enemy which were getting closer and closer by the second, indicating that the British were likely mounting a charge.

A chill went down Warramou's spine as he mulled over what action he should take in response to the situation. He knew that the moment had finally presented itself for him to prove his mettle as a warrior and defender of his beloved people, as Pa Louen had foretold. He had to act decisively against this deadly assault before it was too late. Plucking a poison-tipped arrow from his quiver, he deftly slid it into his bow and then drew it until the string was taut. With the wooden shaft pressed stiffly against his right cheekbone, as his grandfather had taught him as a young boy, he scanned the darkness for signs of the surging line of British troops, a few hundred paces away. Unable to trust his senses, he relied purely on instinct. Like a hunter, he bided his time until he could finally perceive a shadowy movement, then released his deadly projectile into the sea of murk in front of him. Unsure if the arrow had successfully struck its intended target, he grabbed another and readied it for shooting. As he waited to acquire a new mark, he calmly steeled himself mentally for a fight to the death if needed. He promised himself that he would singlehandedly eliminate at least two British soldiers if he were to lose his life in close combat.

Not far away, adjacent to Warramou's position on the battlefield, the situation was equally dire. Duvallé and Chief Chatoyé, were desperately trying to rally their troops to repulse the

154

British onslaught. The suddenness of the attack had left their forces scattered and ill-prepared to mount a coherent resistance. Several of Duvallé's men had been reveling with a captured barrel of rum and were caught without having their arms near at hand.[1] Others, in particular those from Chatoyé's leeward army, had been asleep recuperating from the previous night's long march from Chateaubelair, and were slow to react to the emergent threat. In some cases, the men did not even realize that they were under attack until it was too late to save themselves. Many of them ultimately panicked and fled for their lives into the surrounding woods. Thus, out of the combined army of almost four hundred Garifuna warriors, French revolutionaries, French settlers and slaves, barely three dozen were able to muster arms to stimy the British offensive.

Chief Chatoyé and Duvallé, recognizing that the battle was fast becoming a one-sided rout, tried to devise a plan to turn the tide back in their favor.

"*Brother, we must strike at the British frontline and drive them back down the hill. Otherwise, I fear they'll soon overrun us and we'll lose this high ground,*" urged Duvallé anxiously, as musket shot blanketed their position.

"*Yes, brother. The time has come to take this fight to the British lines and give them no quarter,*" replied Chief Chatoyé with an almost fanatical fervor.

"*What are you suggesting?*" enquired Duvallé with a furrowed brow, as he tried to figure out what plan his brother was concocting in his head.

"*We must draw closer to their line, so that they no longer have time to reload their muskets. Then charge their ranks and engage them in hand-to-hand combat,*" came Chief Chatoyé's emphatic response.

"*How can we pull this off brother? The pressure from their firing is relentless and has us pinned down here. Besides we have so few of the men at our disposal to mount such a charge. Perhaps it's wiser to abandon this position?*" cautioned Duvallé, who was clearly skeptical of his brother's risky plan.

"*We mustn't retreat brother. Not now nor ever. Our ichéiri are potent and will protect us. We are invincible against the British musket balls and bayonets,*" proclaimed Chief Chatoyé as he fingered the black and red beads of the talisman around his neck, as if he was reassuring himself of the supernatural power of his good spirits.

Without waiting for a reaction, he continued, "*Never forget the ancient war cry of the ancestors. Ana, cariná rote! Aucion paparoto mantoro itoto manto! Only we are people! There are no cowards here, nobody gives up, this land is ours! We must never yield to our enemies!*"

Duvallé's lack of conviction was written all over his face, however, he could not find the words in his throat to challenge his brother, let alone the ancestors.

"Don't worry brother. I'll lead the charge! No harm can befall me anyway as I can't be killed by mortal means," assured Chief Chatoyé with a determined look in his eye, that his brother knew meant that he could never be dissuaded.

Chief Chatoyé's outward show of confidence belied his inner doubt. He had in fact recently been worried about the weakness of his ichéiri and the growing strength of his maboyas, his bad spirits. He himself did not fully believe the last words he had spoken to his brother. As he weighed his next course of action, he recalled the disturbing words of the boyez, from earlier that evening:

"Death and destruction will befall us if we attack Kingstown at an inopportune moment. We must wait until the favor of the gods has been restored and the heavens are aligned to our cause."

During his mystical divinations, the boyez had received a troubling omen from the gods.[2] In a trance induced by a foul-smelling herbal concoction, he had observed a blue smoking star, streaking across the heavens.[3] Suddenly, as he looked on there was a brilliant flash of light which cleaved the sky. This produced a billowing cloud of dust, followed by a pillar of fire that cast a reddish glow as far as the eye could see.

There was no doubt in Chief Chatoyé's mind that the boyez' premonition had forebode disaster. What worried him was that the misfortune had manifest itself so soon, and in such a diabolical way. He was confused about why, even after forestalling the attack on Kingstown, when they were on the brink of eradicating the last vestiges of British occupation in Hiroona, they were still facing this catastrophic situation. *What had he done to bring this calamity upon the Garifuna people?* It seemed as if even the gods were turning their backs on their cause.

CH22

~~~

Chief Chatoyé's last words had stunned Duvallé once more into silence. In his gut, Duvallé knew that it was unwise for his brother to spearhead the counterattack in such bleak conditions. At best it would be a frantic stab in the dark and at worse a calamity that he did not dare to contemplate. Yet he was keenly aware that no amount of reasoning would sway his brother once his mind was made. That was how he had always been ever since they were young boys growing up in Grand Sable.

Reluctantly, Duvallé nodded his head in acquiescence, as he finally found his voice:

"As you command General. Shall I give the musketeers the order to lay down covering fire for the charge?"

Clasping Duvallé on the shoulder in affirmation, Chief Chatoyé replied approvingly, *"That's exactly what we need to get us close enough to the enemy frontline to strike!"*

"In this pitch blackness it's all but impossible to know where the enemy lines begin and end. Even if they were under our noses we would hardly be able to see them," exclaimed Duvallé with a tinge of exasperation.

"Nor they us. These dim conditions can also serve to our advantage, brother," countered Chief Chatoyé, calmly disregarding Duvallé's lingering hesitance.

Chief Chatoyé had barely got these words out, before the hair-raising war cry of the British soldiers, "Buaidh no bàs! Victory or death!" could be heard echoing across the battlefield. This gave a clear signal that a bayonet charge on the main barracks, where the two men were hunkered down, was underway. Duvallé, sensing the urgency of the situation, quickly headed off to comply with his brother's orders. Mustering a band of musketeers from their scattered, depleted forces would be no simple task.

At that moment, Alexander, was rushing forth in the forefront of the British charge. Emboldened by a renewed surge of adrenaline, he had strode doughtily across the field of battle with his sword extended, shielded on his left and right by dragoons with their bayonets fixed. In attaining their objective, they ran past several shadowy patches on the ground, marking fallen French and Black Carib combatants, who had been killed or lay on the ground wounded, dying slowly from their fatal wounds. Ever mindful that a threat could emerge at any moment, from any direction, their eyes constantly probed the blackness for danger. Anyone and anything that offered a prospect of resistance was indiscriminately put to the knife and sword.

Initially slow to catch on to the British maneuvering, Chief Chatoyé only grasped what was happening when the British were

160

bearing down on his position. Immediately drawing his rapier, he ran to confront the assailants, accompanied by two of his most trusted lieutenants, Joyette and Lalime, each armed with a tomahawk and a spear in either hand. As he led the way, he exhorted his other troops to join them in defending the barracks against the British assault. Yelling the Garifuna war cry repeatedly at the top of his lungs, while thrusting his sword emphatically in the air: *"Ana, cariná rote! Aucion paparoto mantoro itoto manto! Only we are people! There are no cowards here, nobody gives up, this land is ours!"*

What followed was the most critical engagement of the battle on Dorsetshire Hill and of the war, thus far. Chief Chatoyé, Joyette and Lalime, found themselves locked in hand-to-hand combat with Alexander and half a dozen dragoons and militiamen. Undeterred by being outnumbered, they refused to capitulate nor withdraw to safety, preferring instead to fight to the death.

Alexander, being a skilled swordsman, squared off against Chief Chatoyé, who was renowned for his skills with melee weapons,[1] while Joyette and Lalime fearlessly faced two bayonet-wielding dragoons each.

As the two men dueled, alternately thrusting and parrying the attack of the other, Alexander sized up Chief Chatoyé in the feeble light of the battlefield. What he first noticed was his foe's impressive build. He was a burly, broad-shouldered, tall, massive beast of a man. Apart from that, what struck him most were the

161

precise, fluid movements with which he wielded his sword, constantly threatening to put him under pressure. The controlled fury of his thrusts and deftness of his parries, clearly indicated that he had received some formal training in the art sword fighting. Yet there was something different about him, that he had never encountered previously in a negro. He conveyed himself with a confident bearing and calmly avoided becoming flustered even when Alexander had him on the defensive.

As Alexander pieced his observations together, it slowly dawned on him that his opponent was a combatant of great importance and prestige. He began to suspect that he was battling against none other than the legendary Black Carib paramount chief, Chatoyé, who was well-known for his bravery and fighting prowess. After a flurry of pernicious sword thrusts against his adversary's chest and head, which were adroitly parried, Alexander seized the courage to address him.

"*You him, Chatoyé?*"[2]

"*Yes, of course,*" came Chatoyé's reply, as he parried yet another sword thrust.

It was at this point, that the four dragoons who had by then already brutally dispensed with Lalime and Joyette, thrust their bayonets into Chatoyé's back.[3] Staggered by these unexpected blows, he let out a spine-chilling howl of pain through his clenched teeth.

162

Then he stumbled and fell to his knees gasping desperately for breath. Still clutching his sword in his right hand, he looked up harshly at Alexander. Their eyes locked for an instant in a coldblooded stare. Alexander then took a step towards Chatoyé, all the while maintaining eye contact, before finishing him off with a sharp slash to the jugular, from left to right. The blow cleaved Chatoyé's thick, sinuous neck open, releasing a spurt of blood that gushed out into the air. His body tumbled headfirst to the ground. Without crying out or groaning, he rolled around with his arms flailing about in violent contortions as he breathed his last. After a frightful struggle with death his mangled corpse came to rest in a pool of warm blood at Alexander's feet.

Shocked by his own actions, Alexander gazed upon his fallen foe in disbelief. Dazed, he examined his right hand, which had heaved the sword that had delivered the fatal blow, as if it was an alien organ that did not belong to his body. Slowly it began to sink in that he had just slain the infamous, paramount chief of the Black Caribs. At a stroke, he was mobbed by a swarm of dragoons and militiamen, heaping praise and cheers upon him.[4] For a moment, oblivious to the ongoing orgy of violence, they basked in the demise of the cruel wild negro tyrant that had been terrorizing the Colony with his rebel army of savages, for the past week.

On the opposite side of the battlefield, the mood in the Garifuna and French camps was starkly different. Duvallé had looked on helplessly as his brother's primordial cries confirmed his

163

untimely demise. It was a crushing blow, despite the fact that he knew deep down that Chief Chatoyé's rash gamble was predestined to fail. The loss to their cause was incalculable. Chatoyé was the Garifuna chief who had the best chance of leading their side to victory in the war. Now, that responsibility had unceremoniously shifted to his shoulders. Without further hesitation, Duvallé, in defiance of his brother's orders, gave the signal for the immediate evacuation of Dorsetshire Hill. It was clear to him that retreat was the only way to staunch the heavy losses that the British were inflicting upon their forces.

Much to his chagrin, in their hasty withdrawal, they were compelled to abandon the bodies of Chatoyé as well as other fallen Garifuna warriors and their French allies. Although it was against their custom, it was unavoidable due to the chaotic fog of the battlefield. Once his forces were regrouped Duvallé was determined to avenge his brother's death by unleashing a campaign of violence that the British would not soon forget. Revenge was the only salve that could mollify his pain.

CH23

~~~

At sunrise, Captain Skynner gave the order to abandon Dorsetshire Hill. It was too expansive a location to be held by his band of just sixty men. Before withdrawing to Fort Charlotte, they destroyed the main buildings and set up a new perimeter of military outposts nearer to Kingstown.[1] He hoped this would suffice to stave off the enemy for the time being. Yet deep down he knew it would be a tenuous calm. The British forces were ill-positioned to capitalize on their victory amid the disarray amongst their foes. Casting his gaze blearily towards Kingstown, as he strolled along the leewardmost fortification wall, he pondered the tenuous plight of the capital's beleaguered inhabitants. They would only be out of harm's way as long as the wild negroes and their French allies did not try to bring artillery to bear against them again. Without the timely arrival of more reinforcements, this conflict was clearly destined to become a military quagmire.

Setting these thoughts aside for the moment, Captain Skynner pulled out his white kaolin clay pipe and then casually packed the bowl with a plug of dry tobacco. While gently sucking on the stem, he reached for his brass, pocket tinderbox and pulled out the flint and steel. Then with deft ease he struck the steel repeatedly against the flint to ignite the tobacco until he drew steady puffs of silky white smoke. As he huffed away savoring the intoxicating, sweet aroma, Lieutenant Thompson joined by his side.

"*Good morrow Captain.*"

"*Mornin'. What news, Lieutenant? Are the men ready to clear out?*" Enquired Captain Skynner with an unconcerned look written on his face, his woolly mutton chops quivering gently as he spoke.

"*Aye sir. We'll move off presently. The men are just finishing the burial of the French corpses. May their souls rest in peace.*" The tone of Lieutenant Thompson's voice conveyed a cold detachment as he continued, "*As for the accursed wild negroes, we'll leave their heathen carcasses to rot like wild animals on the battlefield.*"

Pausing for a moment, he languidly let out a yawn while rubbing his weary blue eyes, before coolly changing the subject, "*'Twas an absolutely splendid operation sir. One and a score enemy dead for the loss of just four men and five wounded. I'm sure the Governor'll be well pleased.*"

"*Aye Lieutenant. I reck'n we saved 'is skin dis time. Ought to be wort' at leas' a bloody commendation if he knowed what we done!*" thundered Captain Skynner emphatically. In fact, he secretly hoped to finally secure the promotion to commodore that he rightfully deserved, after being overlooked twice due to his bad temper.

166

"Aye sir! And a barrel of rum and some wenches," added Lieutenant Thompson with a sly grin. He knew full well that the Captain had a weakness for life's pleasures and would surely indulge himself in a carousal after their deployment to St. Vincent was over.

Nodding his head keenly in agreement and bearing an almost toothless smile, Captain Skynner let out a jovial barrel-chested laugh before responding, *"Don't worry Lieutenant, I'll sing our praises far above the stars. The Gov'na'll refuse us nothin'."*

Governor Seton had in fact been already informed by his aide-de-camp of their mission's success. Captain Skynner had sent him a terse missive via a Militia scout not long after the fifteen minute slaughter was concluded.[2] It contained just ten words which captured all he deemed necessary to relay at the time:

Dorsetshire Hill secured. Will occupy till morning.

Captain Lancelot Skynner

Captain Skynner, for his part, was never one to issue lengthy battlefield reports. From past experience he had learned that supplying too many details to superiors often led to disastrous consequences. If the operation failed to achieve its objective, despite the odds, he would have to shoulder the blame. While if it succeeded they would appropriate the credit he deserved, and at best he would garner a doffed hat. For this reason, he preferred to personally debrief the Governor on the outcome of the daring nighttime raid on Dorsetshire Hill. His cryptic message was therefore intended to satisfy the minimum needed to inform Governor Seton while still allowing him to control the narrative.

After receiving word of the British withdrawal from a scout, Duvallé ordered Warramou and several of his most capable men to covertly retrieve Chief Chatoyé's body and those of the other fallen Garifuna warriors so that they could be accorded customary burial rites. Warramou, had volunteered to lead this perilous mission since he felt guilty about the previous night's debacle. He wanted to revisit the scene of the battlefield to piece together what had gone wrong since he was convinced that the rout by the British could have been averted. If only he had just been braver by entering the fray sooner.

In fact, Warramou had narrowly escaped the same fate as Chief Chatoyé. The British bayonet charge had passed within forty paces of his position. In the nearly impenetrable darkness, he could barely make out what was happening from the cacophony of screams, cries and explosions that echoed across the battlefield as his kinsmen were mercilessly massacred by the British dragoons and militiamen.

The return to Dorsetshire Hill was a grisly reminder of the previous night's bloodbath. The pungent stench of death hung in the air as the men combed the summit searching for their fallen kinsmen. Bodies were strewn all around. From the flagstaff, on the leeward side of the hill, to the ruins of the barracks, in the center of the summit, to the southern side of the hill, where the canons

168

had been disabled. Chief Chatoyé's body was found not far from the main barracks, where it had been dragged several dozen paces from the place he had fallen, marked by a pool of black, blood-stained earth. His pulverized corpse was barely recognizable. His skin appeared grey and sallow, and his body bore the tell-tale marks of mutilation. The barbaric British had gouged his eyes out with their bayonets, and pilfered his silver rapier and golden earrings.[3] His face and neck were bruised and battered beyond recognition, so he could only be identified by the tattoos on his arms and legs, and by his tremendous hulk.

Seeing Chief Chatoyé in this sorrowful state brought tears to Warramou's eyes. In that moment, as he struggled to accept this outcome, he recalled the prophetic words of Pa Louen: *"Rise up and embrace your warrior's fate. Lead our people to vanquish their enemy in this just war."* Surely this catastrophe was what Pa Louen had foretold in his dream. It was now his turn, together with Chief Duvallé, to take on the mantle of leadership for his people in this brutal war. Clasping his hands on Chief Chatoyé's breast, he made a solemn oath to Tamosi to fulfil his destiny as a Garifuna warrior by walking in the paramount chief's footsteps.

After ordering his men to prepare the body for removal to Grand Sable, Warramou continued his roving inspection of the battlefield. Near one of the outer fortifications, he stopped dead in his tracks. On the ground, not far from the entrance, lying face-down in a blood-soaked patch of grass was the half-naked body

169

of a young female fighter, of moderate height, with a sinewy frame. From her wounds it was evident that she had been struck in the back by musket fire while fleeing. The trail of blackened blood and trampled grass leading to where she lay indicated that she had tried to crawl away after being hit, but had not made it far before expiring. When Warramou flipped her body over, his jaw dropped. He gasped in surprise as he recognized the handsome, round face staring back at him. The thick, luscious lips and slightly protruding eyes, peeking out from under sharply arched eyebrows belonged to Nanette. For the second time that day his eyes began to water. Overcome with grief and suffocated by the fetid air smothering the battlefield, Warramou quickly gave the order for his men to withdraw.

In the wake of the defeat on Dorsetshire Hill, the Garifuna and French camps were flung into complete disarray. The French revolutionaries, upon learning of Chief Chatoyé's death had largely deserted. In a frenzied panic they had fled towards the Leeward coastal town of Layou in the hopes of being evacuated by ship. On route, amid the havoc of their hasty retreat in the dark, a score of them were captured by a Militia patrol. They were summarily executed by hanging at daybreak as the high tide rolled in.[4] Citoyen Touraille's lieutenant, Citoyen Mather, was among the few who were fortunate enough to evade apprehension. Upon reaching the coast he embarked hastily on a sloop bound for Guadeloupe, with a small party of men, ostensibly to apprise
170

Governor Hugues of their recent defeat and to receive new orders on how to continue the war with their Black Carib allies.[5]

For their part, the Garifuna forces withdrew towards their own country, on the windward portion of Hiroona, confounded and dismayed. Chastened by the defeat in the battle, which had cost the lives of fifteen Garifuna warriors including their paramount chief and general, not to mention inflicted dozens of casualties, Duvallé had only two things on his mind. Mourning the loss of his brother and exacting vengeance against the British. Following the Garifuna custom when a great warrior dies there would be a hiatus in fighting for several days while the dugu funeral ceremony was performed by his kinsmen in bereavement.[6] Duvallé intended to use this lull in hostilities to plot a counteroffensive against the British that he hoped would shift the momentum of the war back in their favor.

CH24

~~~

Alexander tottered unsteadily to the left, then staggered clumsily forward, before collapsing unceremoniously on the ground behind the barracks at Fort Charlotte. He was inebriated after a day of carousing fueled by cheap rum and grog supplied by several wealthy planters. As his face caressed the dew soaked grass that had cushioned his drunken fall, he struggled in vain to get back on his feet, while smiling contentedly to himself. In the past twenty-four hours his life had been upended in the most splendid way. Thanks to his valiant exploits on Dorsetshire Hill, he was now the most revered British man in the colony. Everywhere he went in Kingstown, he heard his name being whispered on the lips of men, women and children. They hailed him as the slayer of the much-dreaded, notoriously savage chief of the wild negroes, Chatoyé. To his amusement, many who were awed by this near superhuman feat, even took a step back as he swaggered past, lest they cross his fearsome path.

His fame had spread like wildfire, in part due to his own machinations. Each time he was asked to recount the story of how he had slain the infamous wild negro chief, he had included new details, embellishing his role even further, while conveniently failing to mention the bayonets that had been thrust in Chief

Chatoyé's back. First he had boasted that he had bested the wild negro chief in single combat following an intense swordfight, in which he had slipped and fell on several occasions. However, he found this version of the story unsatisfying since it failed to portray himself sufficiently as the underdog in the duel. So later he thought better of this and found it more endearing to accentuate his gallantry by describing how he had taken on the wild negro chief and two of his cronies all at once, and defeated them singlehandedly with his deft sword skills. However, his favorite elaboration of all related to the final blow that he had mercilessly delivered to seal Chief Chatoyé's fate. As he recalled it, he had stared the cowering, wounded beast of man in the eyes, and denied his desperate pleas for mercy. When he landed the fatal blow he had with his own eyes seen the vile demon within him cast out. As Chief Chatoyé fell mortally to the ground Alexander had crossed himself and prayed for the repose of the heathen's soul. This latter part added a poetic touch to the story, which found sway with all who heard his tale, especially those of a religious inclination.

Yet Alexander's renown was not confined to the ordinary citizens of the Colony. Even the upper echelons of the colonial society were clamoring after him. Governor Seton, had feted him, along with Captains' Skynner and Campbell, at an extravagant banquet aboard the HMS *Roebuck* attended by Sir William Young, the wealthiest man on the island. Thanks to Captain Skynner showering him with praise, he had been lauded as the savior of the Colony and lavished with promises of immense wealth and prestige beyond his wildest dreams, when the war was over. In addition, the Governor had promoted him forthwith to the rank of major in the Militia,[1] which came with a handsome increase in pay and victuals. The name Leith would henceforth be proclaimed with great pride and honor across every hill and vale in the Colony and beyond. His family name would be finally restored to its rightful place among the landed Scottish gentry. This was the culmination of the dream that he had pursued relentlessly since arriving in the Ceded Isles nearly a quarter of a century prior, with barely a penny to his name.

On top of that Alexander's newly elevated social status accorded him many unwritten privileges, of which he intended to avail himself fully. From booze to women, land and slaves, he was assured that nothing would be denied him. Everyone, from the Governor down to the lowest plantation bookkeeper, now owed him a debt of gratitude for his service to the Colony. He was no longer a worthless nobody, condemned to perpetual penury, that could be cast aside indifferently. What he relished most of all was the respect accompanied by the vertigo of importance that had come with his ascendance. He had always known that he was destined for greatness despite his humble beginnings.

These heady thoughts danced gaily in Alexander's delirious mind as the world around him kept spinning. After several futile
174

attempts he managed to prop himself up on his hands and knees. In his drunken stupor it was impossible for him to regain his feet without assistance. The pounding in his head seemed to be intensifying with each passing moment. It felt as if his brain was being boxed with leaden gloves, and his mind would split open at any moment, spilling out onto the ground before him. In the midst of this delirium, Rosie flitted into his thoughts and he felt a sudden surge of will power to crawl to her shack behind the Anglican church. As he was accustomed, when intoxicated, he longed for the warm caress of her bosom and thighs. Yet his arms and legs defiantly refused to comply. He soon collapsed again to the grass and drifted off into reverie.

Alexander had indeed indulged in a day of debauchery, however, it did not all go as gloriously as he had remembered it. At the banquet in his honor, he had hardly paid attention to Governor Seton's words nor those of the gathered planters. Beyond basking in the congratulatory remarks and adulation he had received, his attention had been occupied elsewhere. One of Sir Young's chamber slaves, a young voluptuous negress, had caught his eye. He quickly found himself plying his charms on her as she supplied him with generous refills of rum and grog.

Had he been more attentive, he would have realized that the Crown was in no position to deliver on the bounteous promises the Governor had made. In spite of their operation's success on Dorsetshire Hill the war was at a critical turning point, which was laid bare by the Governor himself in a conversation with Sir Young, Captain Skynner and Captain Campbell, to which Alexander was privy.

"*Gentleman, we mustn't repose under the shadow of our laurels after last night's victory. This war is not yet won. We shall remain in peril until the last of those wretched wild negroes is exterminated,*" warned Governor Seton sternly.

Continuing his discourse, he added cryptically, "*Captains' Skynner and Campbell have impressed upon me that we lack sufficient manpower to drive home our advantage without putting Kingstown in undue danger. This may force my hand in adopting more drastic measures to combat the enemy.*"

The eyes of Sir Young lit up with curiosity upon hearing the Governor's last words. Surely he thought, Governor Seton, would not dare to do the unthinkable.

"*We may be compelled to arm the slaves to root out the enemy from their stronghold. Till now I have avoided contemplating such a dangerous proposition. However, our present predicament leaves me with few options.*" The Governor paused to allow his words to sink in.

"*Tis indeed a risky venture milord. I'm 'fraid no further reinforcements from Martinique will be fordcoming. Nor from Barbados for da time being. So it strikes me da best option at da mom'nt,*" advised Captain Skynner reassuringly, while nodding his

176

head in approval. His usual jovial demeanor was slightly subdued by the anxious mood pervading the room.

"*Aye! Lest we forget, gentlemen, the disquieting lessons the French have learnt in Guadeloupe and Haiti.[2] Arming slaves and tempting them with the taste of the forbidden fruits of freedom may ring the death knell of slavery and with it our most profitable enterprises will be laid to ruin,*" warned Sir Young with a grim look written on his face. As the wealthiest man in the Colony he, of all the men present, had the most to lose from such a rash decision. Were the Governor's gamble not to pan out, he could easily find himself in dire financial straits.

"*Have no fear Sir Young. I've no plans for hordes of slaves to maraud around the island with muskets and machetes. The Lord knows that'd be tempting fortune,*" clarified the Governor.

Captain Campbell jumped in to support him and further allay Sir Young's fears, "*Lieutenant Thompson, Captain Skynner and Major Leith here, will train up ten score of the most trusted slaves into a regiment. We'll then send 'em into the bush to hunt down those wretched wild negroes. Isn't that right Alexander...*"

As he spoke, Captain Campbell elbowed Alexander in the ribs in a vain attempt to grab his attention. However, Alexander could only muster a vague reply, "*Hmmmmph. Er....what'd you say Captain?*" Before Captain Campbell could respond, he blurted out drunkenly, "*Aye Captain. I'm keen to slay more wild negroes. Just like I slit the throat of the cruel beast himself.*"

177

Alexander, who was by now deeply engaged in his flirtation with the negress, wanted desperately to excuse himself from the present company so that he could move in for the kill. However, he knew, despite his inebriation, that it would be bad form to make an exit until the Governor and Sir Young had taken their leave. So, he resisted his urge to do so and relegated himself to loitering around the men, disinterested in their ongoing conversation.

Satisfied with all that he heard, Governor Seton raised his glass to toast the heroes who had saved the Colony in her darkest hour of need. Although he had misgivings about the approach recommended by his military advisors, he could see no clear alternative. It was the only way that would allow them to fend off the wild negroes and French long enough for reinforcements to arrive from Britain in a few months. Till then it would be a war of attrition, in which they had to keep the enemy on the backfoot. He was sure that it would not take long for them to mount a vicious counterattack in retaliation for Chief Chatoyé's death.

PART IV – Memento Mori

Tooking ma kanari
Minara tanara manaricou
Kimabouisi cana kivacou.

English translation:
Destroyed our strength;
myself without birthright, food or weapon.
Without strength my plants, our land and water;
Without weapons I am destroyed.
Our strength is without defences, fortress or land.

(Anonymous - Carib lament from the records of Fort St. Christian,
St. Thomas, United States Virgin Islands)

CH25

~~~

The loud wailing of women could be heard in every corner of the Black Carib territory. From Owia Bay down to the Byera River a shroud of sorrow and despair was smothering Hiroona, strangling every facet of daily existence. The usual thrum of carefree laughter and mirthful music could no longer be heard echoing through the hills and valleys of the Garifuna heartland. In the aftermath of the fateful battle on the summit of Dorsetshire Hill, life seemed to be waiting with bated breath for destiny to run its diabolical course. The death of paramount chief Chatoyé had dealt a devastating blow to the morale of the Garifuna people.

In Grand Sable, preparations were diligently being made for Chief Chatoyé's dugu. This traditional funerary ceremony would be more elaborate than ever seen before in Hiroona. Every Garifuna warrior would be obliged to come to the village to pay their respects to the greatest chieftain their tribe had ever seen. Chief Chatoyé's voyage into the afterlife would be eased over the course of several nights through a series of intricate rituals and sacrifices performed under the direction of the boyez. The culmination of the dugu ceremony would be the interring of his body in a burial chamber located on a mountain ridge, just beyond the outer limits of Grand Sable, looking out on sacred Mount

Qualibou to the north and on the leeward coast of the island, towards Chateaubelair.[1]

The grave site was a hive of activity. Taking advantage of the lull in fighting, several young warriors, were enlisted to cut a rectangular glade in the dense brush with cutlasses to make room for the large gathering of mourners expected to participate in the burial rites. In the middle of the clearing, the five widowed wives of the paramount chief, Reuma, Barauda, Waruguma, Waroutie and Gulicha, had used digging sticks and their bare hands to excavate the tomb out of the fecund, vermillion earth. In accordance with Garifuna custom, the toil of the women in making the crypt had continued through the night and was not aided by any man. The chamber itself was round in form, measuring about four paces in diameter and was roughly the height of a man in depth.[2] About halfway down the main shaft, the pit widened to form a small inner grotto on one side. To finish it off, the walls and floor of the tomb had been smoothly plastered over with kneaded mud.

On the other side of Grand Sable, straddling the windward coast, the mood at the carbet was heavy. Duvallé sat together with his lieutenants, Warramou, Massoteau and Dufond, mulling over the next steps that the beleaguered Garifuna army would take. A venomous rage was brewing in their hearts which was itching to be released.

"Three days have passed since the battle. It's time for us to show our teeth to the British. Qualeva's vengeance must be visited

on these spineless cowards. I won't rest until my brother's loss, and the deaths of Lalime and Joyette are avenged at least ten-fold!" declared Duvallé, his voice laced with a caustic fire.

"Yes brother, the time for licking our wounds is over. At the urging of the Gods, our hands, righteously armed, shall teach the British a lesson they'll not soon forget. Like our fathers before us," echoed Massoteau, who was raring to fight back.

"All of us stand by you in seeking justice, brother Duvallé. We must scratch their back with agouti teeth and rub salt in their wounds.[3] Only then will they learn to fear the mighty Garifuna!" proclaimed Dufond, goaded by the swollen anger of Duvallé and Massoteau.

"Our scouts have reported that the enemy have set up several defensive outposts nearer to Kingstown. Their current disposition suggests that they're unlikely to attack soon unless they receive further reinforcements. We should seize this opportunity to exact our revenge before it's too late," offered Warramou, his eyes lighting up with feverish excitement as he spoke. Continuing his thought further, he added, *"Why don't we strike near Kingstown and teach them that nowhere is safe from our wrath?"*

"That'll surely come at no small risk, brother. If we go into the snake's den, we should be careful not to get bitten," cautioned Duvallé, who was intrigued by the proposal, but wary of sending his forces into another debacle.

183

"Surely Fort Charlotte is impenetrable. It's thirty-four artillery pieces won't allow us to get close enough to Kingstown to even let off a single musket shot. What exactly are you cooking up Warramou?" enquired Massoteau, with a skeptical frown on his face.

"For now, their fortress is beyond our reach. Yet we can still hurt the British cause by destroying what they hold dear. Let's burn their estates near Arnos Vale to the ground. We'll not leave a blade of unburnt sugar cane from Sion Hill to Calliaqua. Their artillery won't be able to touch us as we'll be well out of their range,"[4] rejoined Warramou undeterred by the doubt written on the faces of Duvallé, Dufond and Massoteau.

"So, what you're proposing is that we set fire to all the sugar estates near Arnos Vale, including Sir William Young's? He was a great friend of Chief Chatoyé and a staunch ally of our people after the last war. We were once dinner guests at his villa," observed Duvallé wistfully.

Without batting an eyelid, Warramou responded with stone-cold conviction, "This is now an all-out war, brother. After Chief Chatoyé's death we can ill afford to leave any stone unturned. You know well that our bonds of friendship with the British have long been strained. There can be no limits to our fight to protect Hiroona."

"What you say is true brother Warramou. It is incumbent on us to do what is necessary to prevail at all costs," affirmed Duvallé,

184

with a gentle nod of his head. He knew all too well that sentimentality had no place in war.

Won over by Warramou's argument, he hesitated no further in giving the order that Warramou had sought, *"Set to work right away planning the attack, Warramou. You are in the lead for this raid. Take twenty of our best warriors to second you."*

"As you command, general. I shan't fail you!"

Looking pensively across the carbet into the eyes of Dufond and Massoteau, Duvallé added, *"Dispatch canoes immediately to the French in Hewanorra and Karukera informing them that we urgently request their support. We must replenish our stockpiles of ammunition, gunpowder and weapons to continue the fight against the British. And we must prepare for the worst. This war may well turn into a long drawn out engagement."*

Dufond and Massoteau nodded their heads in acknowledgement, before turning to leave the carbet, following Warramou.

Meanwhile, as the sun climbed higher, peeking through the cloudy late afternoon sky, Reuma returned to her hut from the gravesite to prepare for the start of the dugu ceremony that evening. Since her husband's death her life had descended into chaos. She could not believe that Chatoyé had died from mortal wounds since she had always believed him to be invincible. His ichéiri had till now faithfully protected him in countless battles dating back to the last war. Arrows, musket balls, boutous and knives had hardly ever left more than a scratch on his body. Reuma was certain this was the work of some dark magic, that not even the boyez could have combatted with his mysterious potions and incantations. This conviction was reinforced in her mind after seeing Chatoyé's mutilated corpse. Overcome with grief, she had wept uncontrollably for days on end, and could only be consoled by her daughter, Ranné. Together, they kept a vigil, over his body, which lay in a hammock slung on poles outside Reuma's hut. Despite being carefully washed, painted red with roucou dye from crushed annatto seeds and wrapped in a clean, white shroud made from cotton,[5] he still appeared like an alien creature that did not belong to her.

In the midst of another bout of sobbing, Ranné came home to check on Reuma. She maintained an impenetrable façade of strength for her mother, despite her own struggle against the crushing weight of her deep sorrow. Hers was a double burden of grief. Compounding the loss of her father, was the looming loss of her mother, which would shatter her world. Everything she held dear in life would be demolished in a fleeting moment. In its place all she would be left with is a bottomless pit of pain and grief. To survive she had already resigned herself to a numb, hollow existence till the end of her days. Memories of love and happiness would forever be buried in the clay pots of her mind, to preserve them like seasoned flying fish and agouti meat.

186

"Mama, you should eat something before the ceremony starts. Don't worry, I'll watch over Papa to protect him from the evil spirits," urged Ranné, who was visibly worried about her mother. She had never seen her this distraught. Not even after her little brother had died of fever as a baby, when she was a little girl. Back then her mother had cried for three days straight before returning to her normal self. However, this time was different. Her mother had stopped eating and drinking, except for the meagre mouthfuls of ereba dipped in water that Ranné had managed to coax her to swallow. She hardly slept, nor did she keep the hut clean as she was accustomed to doing. It was as if she had already surrendered to death.

In a feeble, almost inaudible whisper Reuma answered, "I'm not hungry my child. Watching over him calms my soul. I can feel his presence. He is here with us."

Talking almost to herself, she added dolefully, "Without you Joseph, I cannot go on. My strength is without defense, refuge or hope. I am destroyed."

Cradling her mother's face affectionately in both hands, while wiping away the tears pooling in her swollen eyes, Ranné attempted to comfort her, "We must remain strong Mama. Papa would not have wanted us to give up…Come, let's get you ready for tonight's ritual. I'll do your hair the way papa liked it; with the golden coronet that you wore when you were married."

Yet in that moment, these words of solace fell on deaf ears, as Reuma appeared to be trapped in a delirious trance of grief. She kept rocking back and forth, while mumbling over and over, *"My strength is without defense, refuge or hope. I am destroyed."*

Recognizing that her mother would not soon come out of her torpor, Ranné sighed, picked up the bowl of ereba and water that she had brought to feed her mother, before withdrawing inside the thatched walls of the hut.

Her mother's gaily colored costume for the burial ceremony, seemed strangely out of place for such a somber occasion. Yet it had been made according to the boyez's exacting instructions. Hung up on the thatched wall above her father's favorite boutou, with its intricate geometric etchings, the costume dazzled in the fading light of dusk. She drew closer and grasped the thick slab of mahogany. Squeezing the handle of the boutou tightly, she secretly hoped it would infuse her with the last remnants of her father's powerful life force. As the hour drew nearer she knew that she too would struggle to find the strength needed to live on.

CH26

~~~

A steady stream of male slaves was paraded in front of Captain Skynner and Lieutenant Thompson, near the large, green, wrought iron gates at the entrance to Fort Charlotte. Shirtless and chained at the neck, as if heading to the auction block, their sturdy ebony bodies glistened with sweat in the tropical heat and humidity. As they trudged past, amid the metallic chorus from their jangling shackles, each slave was carefully scrutinized one-by-one for defects that would deem him unfit for military service. The old and infirm were summarily dismissed, along with those with a history of running away. The telltale signs of such disloyalty being plain to see on their mutilated backs, deformed limbs and scarred faces.

To establish a Black Ranger regiment, following Governor Seton's orders, Captain Skynner, together with Lieutenant Thompson, sought to requisition at least two hundred dependable slaves, capable of engaging in guerilla warfare against the Black Caribs. Each conscripted male slave would be duly appraised to a value which would be paid to the slave owner in the event of his death. Their mission would be to venture out into the hinterland of the island, to harass the Black Caribs and destroy their provisions, starving them into submission. At the same time, they would demolish the Black Carib canoes to cut off their smuggling routes to Grenada, St. Lucia and Guadeloupe. This would require the Black Rangers to navigate the almost impenetrable warren of thickly wooded inland passes that guarded the Black Carib Territory; something that no European had ever succeeded in doing while returning alive.

The two naval officers peered at the tide of human flesh flowing by, idly discussing the peculiar challenges imposed by this assignment from the Governor.

"From the looks of this lot I reckon we 'ave a 'erculean task on our 'ands, Lieutenant. 'ow we're s'pose to whip dis crud into shape is beyon' me? The Gov'na knowed that'd be a longshot eh!" observed Captain Skynner skeptically, lacking his usual barrel-chested, jovial tone.

"Aye sir. For aught I know these slaves might cross us by joining forces with the enemy. That'd surely turn the scales against us in this war," replied Lieutenant Thompson flatly. His beady blue eyes gently waltzing as he spoke.

"ere's indeed a wee chance that might 'appen. If yuh ask me da real shame of it all is da bloody greed. Tis pure extortion, Lieutenant. I'd pay no more than a song for dis rabble o' slaves. The landlubbing planters 'ere are worse than bloody thiefing buccaneers!" offered the Captain while sucking his teeth disapprovingly. As he spoke he shot a glance at one slave in particular who seemed to carry himself differently from the rest. He
190

was a short, stocky, middle-aged but young-looking man who had a confident, slightly haughty bearing. His distinctive tribal scars imprinted on his cheeks like whiskers and his self-assured disposition, made him standout from the usual dreary-eyed, defeated slave who traipsed by, which had caught Captain Skynner's keen attention.

"Hmmmph. Perhaps I spoke too soon Lieutenant. Dere goes a fine 'un. 'e might do us well to lead dis sorry bunch into battle."

Calling him over for closer inspection the Captain enquired, *"What's yuh name boy?"*

"Koanda, at yuh service milord. De Governor been send me fe yo." As he spoke he affected a low obsequious bow, which he often employed to ingratiate himself to his European masters.

"Very well Kowanda. Me and muh associate 'ere wuz jus' thinkin,' perhaps yuh might be da one we're on da lookout for to lead dis ragged lot. A lad who's a fearluss leader, if yuh know whad I mean." explained Captain Skynner who had been quickly disarmed by Koanda's servility.

"Yessuh. I's yuh man. Jus' tell me wat yo wan' me fe do. Me no 'fraida dem Black Caribs. Nevah dat!" The wide, toothy servile grin on his face was sufficient for the two naval officers to confirm his selection as a sergeant in the Black Rangers.

Governor Seton had in fact volunteered Koanda's services to the Black Ranger force in the secret hope that he would keep

191

an eye on the slaves. Given the great risk involved, he wanted to have a finger on any emergent threat of disloyalty amongst the slaves. Koanda, being his most dependable house slave would be a perfect plant. For his part, Koanda was well suited for this role since he had long convinced himself that Europeans were far too powerful to ever be defeated by lowly, artless African slaves or wild negroes. He saw no point in waging a hopeless fight against an insurmountable, superior enemy such as the British. However, he did see considerable personal advantage for himself by assuming a key role in the inevitable quelling of the Black Caribs. It would ingratiate himself further to the Governor while offering him greater standing amongst his fellow slaves. He secretly hoped that if he excelled in his role, he might even be offered a substantial financial reward. Perhaps a sum of money that could lead to the fulfilment of his dream. Although it was a long shot, and he was already well past the prime of his life, he longed to one day be manumitted. He had in fact already been saving up for over seven years to buy his freedom.

Pleased with himself, Koanda strutted off towards the Governor's quarters to share his good fortune with all who would listen. He relished any chance to elevate his social status amongst his peers.

Unbeknownst to Koanda, there was one glaring flaw in the Governor's plan to mobilize the Black Rangers. He had mostly concerned himself with the financial interests of the slave owners.

It had not crossed the Governor's mind to consider the motivation for the slaves themselves to remain loyal to the Crown beyond their innate hatred of the Black Caribs as dreaded catchers of runaway slaves. Many slaves had legitimate grievances to incentivize them to fight against the British due to their habitual overwork, harsh punishment and squalid living conditions. Only vague promises would be made to the slaves regarding the compensation that they would receive for their wartime service. Apart from an extra half-ration of salted pork per week, and ostensibly the time off from working in the cane fields and sugar mills, when they were hunting down the wild negroes, they would be offered little else by way of monetary reward.

With Koanda's departure, Captain Skynner lost interest once again in the dreary procession of slaves. He attempted to alleviate his boredom by lightening the mood.

"*Did yuh see Major Leith yet dis morn, Lieutenant? He shoulda bin 'ere to help us inspeck dis sorry lot. Lord knowed he wuz confound'dly jaked when las' I seen 'im by da ball yesternight. 'e could barely walk straight.*"[1] The Captain let out his trademark infectious barrel-chested laugh, which made his paunch shake like flummery pudding as he ridiculed Alexander for his intoxication, on the previous night.

"*Aye. Poor sod. I heard a couple o' lads found him convulsing on the ground behind the barracks over yonder. He was muttering some drunken rot about chasing some negro wench or the other,"* sneered Lieutenant Thompson with a slightly bemused grin on his face. As he spoke, he gestured behind his shoulder vaguely indicating where Alexander was last seen retching.

"There's a lad who enjoys 'im some grog and houghmagandie,[2] *ehh! Lord knowed yuh can' blame 'im for chasin' a good romp when 'e's soused,"* chuckled Captain Skynner, who himself had a healthy penchant for debauchery. While saying these words, he took out his kaolin pipe and a plug of dry tobacco to satisfy his midmorning smoking fix.

On the other side of Fort Charlotte, Governor Seton was sitting at his waxed-honey colored kneehole desk pondering his next move. He had just written orders for the execution of several traitors; among them four Marriaqua Yellow Caribs and a handful of French settlers.[3] They would be hanged at dawn the next day as punishment for their treasonous acts against the Crown in aiding and abetting the Black Caribs in their recent incursion into Kingstown. One Frenchman had in fact been caught red-handed with a letter urging Governor Victor Hugues to send an invading armada from Guadeloupe to seize Kingstown before the British forces were replenished. The Governor, was certain there would soon be more mischief afoot. He wondered how long the Colony could hold out against the wild negroes. Like a wounded beast, after the death of Chief Chatoyé, they were now more dangerous than ever.

194

However, Governor Seton recognized that all of the actions he had taken thus far were reactionary. In the long run, he needed to find a permanent solution to the wild negro problem in St. Vincent, otherwise the Colony would perennially be threatened. As he wrestled with what to do next, he recalled the conversation he had with Josephine, the previous night. It had stuck with him, churning in his head all morning.

While brushing her long, silky mane of curly, black hair as she often did before going to sleep, she had brought up a subject that had been bedeviling him over the past few days.

"You know what you ought to do James. After this war is over you need to get rid of those wretched wild negroes once and for all. If you don't then every few years they'll make trouble for us." Josephine spoke these words with the conviction of someone who knows that what they are saying is obvious even to a buffoon.

"What are you suggesting my bonnie?" replied Governor Seton with a tinge of curiosity in his voice. Normally, he avoided discussing such political topics with Josephine since he felt it was inappropriate for his lover to meddle in the politics of the Colony. However, on this occasion he indulged her, since her comments had piqued his interest.

She sniffed the delicious aroma of the coconut oil that she had rubbed into her hair earlier, as she responded bluntly.

"If it were up to me I'd round up every last one of those savages and ship 'em off to a land far away where they could

195

never think of coming back to St. Vincent." Her face twisted into an ugly scowl revealing all too plainly her disdain for the Black Caribs.

"But how? I'm not sure I've got the authority to take such a drastic action. Besides, where should I send them to? Such a war-like tribe of people would surely cause problems anywhere they go," pondered the Governor aloud.

Setting the hair brush down gently, she turned to look at the Governor with a puzzled frown, before gently chiding him.

"It doesn't matter James. You're the Governor. You have the power! Just make a decree or whatever you need to do to make it happen. Surely, every planter on this island will be behind you."

"Yes, you're quite right my bonnie. It's the only way we can wrest the fertile part of this island from those savages. Besides it was they who broke the treaty not us. So, we've every right to do as we see fit. To such an enemy I cannot apply the laws of war. We must exact on them the same treatment which our countrymen who are prisoners receive from them.[4] The only answer is to exterminate this savage and merciless race of Caribs, with whom no treaties are binding, no favors conciliating nor any laws divine or human restraining."[5]

The seed which had been subtly planted in his mind by Josephine was now germinating. The Governor decided to immediately draft a letter to the Crown proposing the deportation

196

of the Black Caribs at the end of the war.[6] He requested funds for a suitable location to be identified and purchased, and for a convoy of ships to be outfitted for the transport of several thousand men, women and children. His justification to London for this severe punishment was straightforward. The Black Caribs had committed numerous acts of treachery, murder and treason, while also violating the treaty with Britain. He expected little sympathy in London for the Black Caribs as they had been a thorn in the side of British interests in St. Vincent from the very beginning.

Although it comforted him greatly to write this missive, Governor Seton was keenly aware that the war was far from over. Victory for Britain was not yet assured. So it was wise for him not to get ahead of himself in dreaming of the extirpation of the Black Caribs on the island. He knew all too well that a hefty price would be paid for underestimating their intransigence.

CH27

~~~

A heavy downpour of rain greeted the start of the final ritual of the dugu ceremony. Fittingly, the heavens above Hiroona were weeping in commiseration with the grieving Garifuna tribe. Yet it was a peculiar rainfall. It was as if the clouds had refused to relinquish their moist nectar for a long time, like pent up emotion, until they had finally burst, amid loud claps of thunder, releasing a deluge of liquid anger and grief. The warm, heavy raindrops stung the ground as they fell from above, mingling with the dusty, reddish earth to form rivulets like thick veins of blood streaming in all directions.

Unperturbed by the sudden torrent, the mourners poured into the glade forming a wide circle around the burial chamber, outlined by a ring of flaming torches. The boyez, who was at the center, standing atop a mound of loose earth near the mouth of the crypt, was dressed as usual in an assortment of manicou skins, shark teeth and coral talismans. Together with his shock of grey hair and thick, salt and pepper beard, he appeared almost prophetic in the flickering torchlight, as he presided over the burial ceremony. He gave a signal by clenching his right fist while muttering a mysterious chant. It was then that the assembled warriors, in unison, broke into song and dance. Over a hundred bass voices sang the battle songs of the Garifuna, while putting on an impressive dancing display, wielding spears and boutous in mock warfare. Outfitted in full combat attire, the warriors looked resplendent with their faces and bodies glistening with red and black roucou paint in the weak flamelight.

Amid the booming percussion of drums, Chatoyé's limp body, wrapped in a shroud, was borne solemnly in a hammock, from Reuma's hut to the burial site, by an honor guard of six of the most decorated Garifuna warriors. Among them were his brother Duvallé, Massoteau, and Dufond. Their painted faces appeared bleak and emotionless as they wended their way through the glade. Upon reaching the burial crypt, Chatoyé's corpse was carefully lowered into the pit and placed upright in a sitting posture, facing the direction of the rising sun. His body was propped up as if he was squatting around a fire, with his elbows, resting on his knees, and his palms supporting his cheeks.[1] One by one, his most prized possessions were lowered into the grotto of the chamber and positioned around him. His favorite boutou, spear, shield and musket were arranged at an arm's length from him, along with clay pots containing water, seasoned agouti meat and flying fish, ereba, cassava beer and guifiti.[2] All of which were essential to sustain and protect him in his journey into the afterlife.

The boyez clenched his right fist a second time, uttering another incomprehensible incantation, which was followed by the blowing of a lambis. This abruptly signaled the end of the singing

199

and dancing, and a subduing of the drums. He then took a step forward beckoning the chosen pair of Chief Chatoyé's wives. Reuma and Waroutie, dressed in their long, colorful red and green festive costumes, were escorted in single file by the honor guard to the brink of the tomb. A lone torch burned in the burial pit, casting an eerie shadow on the impassive faces of the boyez, and the two women.

The boyez produced a small, dried calabash gourd, containing a potion, which he gave the women to drink.[3] Reuma and Waroutie imbibed it readily, alternately taking long draughts of the noxious fluid until it was completely consumed. While waiting for the concoction to take effect the boyez motioned, with a sweeping gesture of his hands, for the women to address the crowd of mourners.

The first to speak was Waroutie, the youngest of Chatoyé's wives. Tall in stature and elegant in countenance, she appeared ethereal in her colorful costume with her cheeks, forehead and lips painted black and white, in an ornate constellation of circular and rhombic symbols. Her melodic voice carried in the gentle wind as she uttered her final words:

"Noble chiefs, valiant warriors and dear friends, before the dead and heaven above, I call upon you and all of Hiroona to bear witness to my sacrifice. Now, I die for my beloved Chatoyé, the bravest warrior our blessed land has ever seen. In death I shall faithfully escort him as we journey together down the river of the

afterlife in the canoe prepared by the ancestral spirits. I bid thee all farewell!"

After these words left her mouth, Waroutie fearlessly leapt into the pit to join by Chief Chatoyé's side. This act elicited a burst of raucous cheers and jubilant shouts from the approving crowd.

Next, it was Reuma's turn. She stepped forward to the mouth of the pit, wearing the festive, blood-red and forest-green colored loin-cloth and matching top prescribed by the boyez. Her face, like Waroutie's, was elaborately made up with mystical patterns. Reuma's neck, arms and legs were covered with colorful necklaces, bracelets and anklets made of coral and bone, which made a soft rattling noise when she moved. Capping off her funerary outfit, was the lustrous, golden coronet adorning her hair. Even in the frail torchlight it gleamed, suffusing her with a regal bearing, making her appear like a veritable Garifuna queen.

Gazing tenderly down at her deceased husband, Reuma said her last:

"*Chatoyé, most noble chief and lord, your favorite and most loyal wife, Reuma follows you. Qualeva shall reap revenge on my behalf for the foul deed committed by our enemies that deprives Hiroona of her bravest son. I go gleefully wherever thou art. Leave me not behind. In death as in life we shall never be parted. Our souls are forever entwined.*"

Looking up and turning to face the crowd around her, she added finally, *"I bid adieu to you all and to this life."*

201

While Reuma spoke, a cocoon of silence had descended upon the crowd of mourners. She had delivered these words unwaveringly, without a hint of sorrow in her voice nor the shedding of a single tear. In stark contrast to her earlier distraught state, she had exuded poise and calm.

As Waroutie had done previously, Reuma flung herself into the grave after she spoke. She then knelt down at Chatoyé's feet and laid her head on his cold breast in a final loving embrace, peacefully awaiting her fate.

No sooner had Reuma done this than the potion's sleeping effect began to take hold.

Without losing a moment, the boyez addressed the gathering to bring the burial ceremony to a close.

"Let the will of the Gods now be fulfilled. We beseech the ancestors to escort Chief Chatoyé and his wives, Waroutie and Reuma, peacefully on their voyage into the afterlife and to ward off all evil spirits and death's demons. We invoke Qualeva to visit His violent wrath upon the enemies of Hiroona a thousand-fold to avenge this death."

With a solemn bow of his head, the boyez indicated that the burial chamber should be filled. Several strong-armed warriors equipped with hoes and eager hands immediately sent the mound of loose earth cascading down upon Waroutie and Reuma, entombing them alive with their dead husband. In scarcely a few moments the pit was brimmed, with hardly a trace of its existence
202

remaining. The greatest warrior the Garifuna nation had ever known was finally laid to rest.

In a blink of an eye the crowd of mourners dispersed. Scattering in all directions, they vanished with lightning speed as though they were being chased by the vengeful doom of death, leaving the burial site enveloped in a blanket of darkness.

Everyone fled the scene of the burial except for Ranné. She lingered behind to bid farewell to her mother and father. Teary eyed and visibly agitated, she stood silently over the mound marking where her parents lay, grappling with her devastating double loss. In a few fleeting moments everything in the world that had mattered most to her had vanished. The violent shock of seeing her mother buried alive before her eyes had jarred her into a new reality which she was struggling to apprehend. Although she had known this day would come, she was ill-prepared for the blunt trauma that the funeral ceremony had inflicted on her fraught soul. She felt hollow, as if everything inside of her had been broken; shattered into countless tiny fragments, which she could never piece together again. In its place, a chasm of emptiness had opened up within her, which could never be filled.

Ranné shuddered. The coolness of the soft, silky mud squishing between her toes sent a shiver through her spine. Kneeling down, she hunched over the grave, pressing her left cheek against the mushy ground while listening in vain for the last gasping breaths of her mother. Yet only the dull droning pulse of the Earth came to her ears. Her heart trembled with fear as she was transfixed in that moment by the realization that she was an orphan. It swept over her like a violent wave crashing against the rocky shore of her mind. From that moment on, Ranné knew her life would never be the same.

CH28

~~~

The glowering fire in the coals of Susan's eyes was enough to stop Governor Seton dead in his tracks. Despite her petite stature and quiet, unassuming bearing, it was clear from the Governor's awkward posture that he was intimidated by her presence. He tried to avert his gaze as she strode calmly past him in the dimly lit passageway, outside his chambers, but it was impossible to break her hypnotic leer. It made him feel uneasy in his own skin. Although, Susan observed this she didn't say a word. She just kept glaring at him with a piercing stare that seemed to see right through him. Governor Seton deduced immediately that she knew that he had broken their tacit truce. He had brazenly allowed his mistress back into his bed the past few nights. It was no secret. The entire fort knew that the Governor had cast aside his wife for a mulatto slave woman. The untold shame it had brought upon Susan had thrust her even more into the fringes of colonial society, where she was already confined to an almost invisible existence.

Yet the fury smoldering in Susan eyes made it clear that her spirit was far from broken. She obstinately refused to accept being relegated to ignominy by the selfish, philandering impropriety of her husband. As a daughter of the House of Moray, of Abercairney in Scotland,[1] she was determined to uphold her family's noble name. For the hundredth time, she wished she had never fallen for his charms as a young woman. Ambitious men like the Governor, would inevitably outgrow their wives, her sister had once warned her during their courtship. Their insatiable lust for power, wealth and recognition would ultimately consume them and lead to their downfall. They would become easy prey for degenerate vixens like Josephine, who, lacking pedigree or even social standing by wealth, were adept at climbing the social ladder on their backs. As much as she despised Governor Seton for his infidelity and fake piety, she detested her former chambermaid even more. Upstart women like her were the scourge of dignified society. There was no scroll that could be charged with punishments that she did not deserve. Susan longed desperately to see the Governor fall from grace along with his good-for-nothing mistress. She prayed for a way to exact revenge to repay them for the hellish nightmare that her daily life had become.

Governor Seton could hardly imagine the malevolent thoughts stewing in Susan's mind in the moment that their paths crossed. Seeing the flicker of anger in her eyes had perturbed him, not because he perceived a sinister threat from her, but rather due to the very sight of her, which repulsed him, as it was an inconvenient reminder of her wretched existence and his lack of virtue. He was impervious to how she felt, since he had long since relegated her to the confines of the darkest caverns of his mind.

206

He had written her off as a mere afterthought, which he hoped to rid himself of as soon as possible.

As Governor of the Colony, Susan could do him no harm anyway. Her empty threats to inform her family back in Scotland of his adultery, posed a greater risk to her reputation than to his. Given his favor with the Crown, it would at worse be a meaningless scandal quietly swept under the rug by more pressing issues like the war against the Black Caribs. For Susan, it would be far more devastating. The ineffable shame it would bring upon her prestigious family name he was sure would be devastating to her already fragile psyche. Although he bore her no malice, at least not which he admitted to himself consciously, the Governor desired nothing more than for her to extricate herself from his life entirely. Once the war was over he would contrive to ship her off indefinitely to her sister in Barbados. The only thing hindering him from acting sooner was his beloved son, Robert.

After the encounter with Susan, Governor Seton headed to his chambers, tangled in his thoughts. He replayed in his head the meeting he had earlier that day, with Captain Skynner, Lieutenant Thompson and his aide-de-camp, on the precarious security situation in the Colony, which had left him equally unsettled.

"We've received some grave news dis morning Gov'na. Da enemy, after a brief hiatus, has resumed dere attacks. Wast night near Cawwiaqua, despite coming under fire from our guns, dey burned several pwantations and cane fields to da ground. Among

dem was regrettabwy Sir Young's, Viwwa Estate. Dere's reasonable suspichon dat dey are preparing to mount more attacks soon," reported Lieutenant George somberly. He avoided eye contact as he spoke, since he didn't want to see the disappointment written in the Governor's eyes.

Governor Seton was shocked by all he heard, especially since he had assumed that the Black Caribs had been severely weakened by the death of Chief Chatoyé and the flight of their French allies. He had not expected them to regroup so quickly. Interestingly, the news of the destruction of Sir Young's estate did not upset him in the least. In fact, he was strangely pleased that Sir Young, had suffered such a loss at the hands of his one-time friends, the Black Caribs. From his perspective it was advantageous that this event had occurred since Sir Young, might have presented an obstacle to his plans to get rid of the Black Caribs for good at the war's conclusion. Now he would be more amenable to deporting them and perhaps might even convince other planters to support him. This was a most unexpected stroke of luck, which he hoped to capitalize on in due course.

Before the Governor could open his mouth to react to Lieutenant George's report, Captain Skynner jumped in: *"Aye Governor, it seems pretty clear dat dem wild negroes is far from spent. Lord knowed what dey'd do nex'. Unless we..."* His booming voice trailed off ominously as he uttered these last words.

"*Unless we do what? What are you trying to get at Captain?*" probed the Governor. His brow had become furrowed and his lips pursed, revealing the uneasy feeling that he had about what the Captain was about to propose.

"*Unless we take da fight to 'em milord.*" With a wink at Lieutenant Thompson, who was standing nearby, he added, "*We wuz thinkin' las' night about attacking 'em at dere home ground. Till now we've been engagin' dem on our domain.*"

"*That's precisely the purpose of the Black Ranger regiment, isn't it Captain? So what are you implying?*" retorted the Governor, somewhat defensively.

"*Tis true yuh 'xcellency. Dem negroes are a gnarly, inexperienced lot. Lickin' 'em into shape is a right large order. We was thinkin' of someting more impacful...if yuh follow my drif'.*" The mischievous twinkle in Captain Skynner's eyes offered an inkling into the plan he and Lieutenant Thompson had conjured up.

"*Me and da lieutenant over 'ere was thinking dat we could attack 'em deep in dere territory at Owia Bay on da windward coast.[2] We seen it on da way over 'ere from Martinique. We reckon dat we could take it from da coast. Dat'd weaken 'em majorly an' cut off dere smuggling routes to St. Lucia and Guad'loupe.*"

"*Aye Captain. We could it pull it off with the Zebra's crew and a small contingent from the Militia. It should be a standard assault. If we run the ship close under the walls,[3] just like in the raid last year when we took Fort Saint Louis,*"[4] offered Lieutenant Thompson, his beady blue eyes beaming with excitement.

"And what about Kingstown? If this daring operation doesn't go well, it could spell disaster for the defense of the capital. I am unsure it's wise to make such a bold move at this time gentlemen. The risks are just too high," cautioned the Governor, searching both men's faces for a sign they comprehended the gravity of the situation.

"We're positive we can succeed milord. Just like we did at Dorsetshire Hill against da odds," gushed Captain Skynner, who gave an assured, almost smug smile, which masked any doubts that he might harbor.

"Gramercy. Thank you, gentlemen for sharing this plan. Let me mull over this proposal for a few days. I'll send word when my mind is made," responded the Governor evenly. He then gave each man a firm handshake, before dismissing them.

Despite his reservations, deep down, Governor Seton knew the war could not wait. Bold action was required to preserve the Colony. He just did not know if the timing was right. He was tempted by the success on Dorsetshire Hill to believe that the Black Caribs could be defeated in a fortnight, if sufficient force were brought to bear. However, in the near term the Colony was desperately short of manpower. This left him no choice other than to be pragmatic and conserve his scant military resources.

In his chambers the Governor found Josephine anxiously awaiting his return. She greeted him with unexpected exuberance.

"Oh James, I'm so glad you're here! I've had such an awful day," whined Josephine, before affectionately planting a kiss on his neck.

"What's wrong my bonnie?" replied the Governor softly, while looking at her with a concerned look. He could read from the way her top lip quivered slightly as she spoke, that she was agitated.

"That horrid, brutish chamber slave of yours, Koanda. The nerve of him!... He deserves to be sentenced to a hundred lashes and locked in a hotbox for a week!" Without pausing for a reaction from the Governor, she continued her rant, *"He came around the servants' quarters this morning bragging about being commissioned a sergeant in the Black Rangers. Like he's a big wig now? Hmmmph."*

The concerned look on Governor Seton's face revealed that he was sympathetic to what Josephine was saying, yet he was struggling to find the right words to comfort her. This was partly due to his own complicity in sending Koanda to join the Black Ranger's regiment so that he could spy on the conscripted slaves.

Misinterpreting his silence for disinterest, Josephine persisted in her verbal indictment of Koanda, intent on winning the Governor over to her side by shocking him into submission. *"And do you know what else he said James? He boasted that he plans* to buy his freedom after this dreadful war is over! God forbid that Koanda could be running around this island free, like one of those wretched wild negroes. What a disaster that'd be!"

The indignant look that Josephine wore on her face as she spoke these last words made Governor Seton hold his tongue once more.

"And you know what was the worst thing, James? After all that, he had the gall to threaten to put his hands on me. Can you believe that? That ugly, dark as sin brute daring to touch me. Never! You need to put that negro in his place, James." She wagged her index finger scoldingly at the Governor, before bursting into tears. She hid her face in her tiny hands as she sobbed unconsolably.

Cradling Josephine gently in his arms, the Governor, attempted to comfort her by fondly caressing her neck with his spindly hands, as he whispered soothingly in her ear, "Fear not my bonnie. I'll make sure they're no free negroes left in this Colony once this infernal war is over. As for Koanda, he'll never dare lay a finger on you. If he only tries I'll make him a eunuch, so help me God!"

212

CH29

~~~

Ranné sauntered slowly back home from the burial site, down the muddy, steeply sloping mountainside leading to Grand Sable, alone in the pitch blackness. As she approached her mother's hut, from a distance, she could make out a large crowd of mourners milling around the compound. Their torches bathed every corner of the hut in bright orange and yellow shafts of light, giving the thatched walls, composed of faded palm fronds and cachibou leaves, a surreal otherworldly appearance, that was barely recognizable. Equally unfamiliar, was the big wooden spit, attended by several young men, which had been erected near the front of the hut, on one side. Even from a long way off the pleasing charred aroma of the grilled iguana and flying fish filled the cool night air, mixing with the fragrant, intoxicating vapors of the tafia, guifiti, and cassava beer, circulating freely amongst the crowd. Completing the festive scene of the wake, in honor of her deceased parents, were the cheerful sounds of revelry, reverberating rhythmically in all directions. As she drew closer Ranné spied several old men, sitting around on wooden stools entertaining the carousers by merrily playing catchy melodies on their drums and reed flutes. This led many men and women alike to break exuberantly into song and dance, jubilantly gyrating and shuffling their feet back and forth, as they crooned at the top of their lungs.

The celebratory air of the wake contrasted starkly with Ranné's dark mood. Unperturbed by this incongruity, she trundled on mindlessly putting one foot after the other to reach her destination. Even after she emerged into the torchlight, from the shadows of the dense forest surrounding Grand Sable, no one seemed to take notice of her presence. In her bleak state of mind, she appeared more like a ghost than someone walking amongst the living. Despite this, the crowd parted, allowing her to make her way unmolested towards the entrance of her mother's hut, where final preparations were well underway for the climax of the evening. Before Ranné could set foot on the hut's threshold, she was accosted by two elderly women with thick braids of grey hair, dressed in matching yellow and black, cotton loin cloths and tops. Their faces were adorned in an elaborate constellation of symbols and patterns, drawn in red and black roucou dye, and their bodies were decorated from head-to-toe in colorful necklaces, bracelets and anklets made from coral and bone.

Without saying a word, the women led Ranné by the hand to a nearby, low-slung mahogany, stool, on which they induced her to sit. A third elderly woman, similarly attired to the others, soon appeared carrying a shiny, pearly white implement in her left hand. While the two other women forcefully bowed Ranné's head, the third woman firmly grabbed Ranné's long, wavy black hair from

214

behind, pulling it back tightly in a bunch until the roots were exposed. All the while Ranné offered no resistance nor did she utter a single word to the women. The third woman then made a rapid grating action with the pearly white implement, which was briefly illuminated in the flood of torchlight, revealing two fist-sized, sharpened cockle shells.[1] A thick lock of silky black hair soon fell at Ranné's feet. The third woman repeated this action over the course of several minutes until Ranné's head was completely shaven. The three elderly women then released Ranné from their grasp, and allowed her to lift her head up, while she sat limply on the stool.

Surveying the world around her anew, Ranné experienced a bizarre sensation. An intoxicating mixture of fear and relief overcame her. With her hair removed, she felt naked and exposed to the vast, imposing wave of sorrow washing over her. Yet at the same time she was strangely relieved. The yoke of the unbearable grief that she wore within her heart was now visible for all to plainly see. The physical reminder of her deep loss symbolized by cutting off her hair,[2] made her feel free from the burden of suppressing the torrent of emotional anguish surging violently within her. For the first time she allowed herself to fully grieve without shame. Without needing to pretend to be strong for someone else. She began to weep uncontrollably. A flood of warm tears streamed down her cheeks onto the ground, accumulating in puddles of hair and eye water at her feet.

After a long stretch of silence in which Ranné steeled herself for what she was expected to do next, she stood up woodenly. With all eyes fixed on her, she strode forth, boldly snatching a nearby torch from its perch. Amid a din of cheers from the crowd she held the flame against the parched thatch wall of the hut until it caught fire. The blaze quickly spread engulfing the entire compound in a brilliant conflagration that lit up the night sky. Stunned by this final act of destruction, Ranné stood frozen in her tracks helplessly watching the remnants of everything she had known in her life go up in smoke. All that she had left now were the fragments of memories from the past that she would try desperately to preserve in the clay pots of her mind.

As she stared into the flames, in the throes of paralysis, out of the corner of her eye, Ranné spotted Warramou. She could feel the burning coals of his eyes peering at her. Although, she did not turn around to return his gaze she was grateful that he was close by. His mere presence stimulated every fiber in her being. Warramou was the only person alive that she knew would be able to comprehend how she felt at that moment. She knew well that the death of his younger brother, Lorain, had devastated him. But she was loathe to speak to him nor seek his comfort. The door to her heart, which had previously been ajar, was now permanently shuttered as she entered this new chapter of her life.

Warramou, who had been lurking in the shadows observing all that had transpired, stepped out into the light. He was drawn, like a moth to the flame, by Ranné's dazzling beauty in the torchlit night. He wanted desperately to go to her, yet he could sense that there was something peculiar in her bearing, which he had never encountered previously. A cold detachment was written in her eyes and in the hardened lines of her tear-stained face. Beneath this outer façade he could see her darkness. Although it did not scare him away, he perceived, in that moment, that she was best left alone. For a split second, he second-guessed himself. Briefly, he contemplated rushing to her side to comfort her in his arms. However, he quickly thought better of it. Downcast at his own uselessness, he reluctantly turned away.

Before stalking off into the darkness towards Owia, Warramou stole a last loving glance at Ranné. He savored this parting image of Ranné, drinking in every vivid detail to preserve it in his memory for posterity. For he knew in his heart that he would never see Ranné again. Not even if this diabolical war would end in triumph over the British. Yet he was certain of one thing. No matter what would happen, she would never be far from his thoughts, like his grandfather, Pa Louen.

Soli Deo Gloria[3]

Notes

Page vii
1. Perfidious Albion is a pejorative phrase used within the context of international relations and diplomacy to refer to alleged acts of diplomatic sleights, duplicity, treachery and infidelity (with respect to perceived promises made to or alliances formed with other nation states) by monarchs or governments of England in their pursuit of self-interest. Perfidious Albion translates loosely as "Treacherous England."
2. Vae Victis is Latin for "Woe to the conquered." It means that those defeated in battle are entirely at the mercy of their conquerors and should not expect or request leniency.
3. Memento Mori is a Latin phrase meaning "Remember that you must die." It is intended to serve as a reminder of the inevitability of death.

PART I: Perfidious Albion

CH1
1. A boyez is a traditional shaman.
2. Qualeva is the demon God of the Caribs.
3. Hiroona is the indigenous Carib name for the island of St. Vincent.
4. Wai'tukubuli is the Carib name for the island of Dominica.
5. Camerhogne is the indigenous Carib name for the island of Grenada.
6. Obi is the Carib god of weather and storms.
7. Tamosi is the creator god of the Caribs.
8. Ichéiri are good spirits.
9. A pirogue is a large dugout canoe with capacity of up to sixty men, which were used by the Garifuna (i.e., Black Caribs) during raids.

CH2
1. Calliaqua and Carapan are villages in the south of St. Vincent.
2. The first Brigand's War began in St. Lucia on April 1st, 1794.
3. On Feb 21st, 1795 a battalion of British troops was defeated by a group of rebels led by Victor Hugues in St. Lucia.
4. Hasty Pudding and sweet bohea tea were commonly served for breakfast in the late 18th century.
5. Pearl White (later called 'pearlware') porcelain was a popular substitute for China porcelain used by the middle and upper classes in the latter half of the 18th century.

218

6. The "vapors," also known as "hysteric fits," was a mental, psychical, or physical state, related to ungovernable emotional excess or to a temporary state of mind or emotion. It was ascribed primarily to women and thought to be caused by internal emanations (vapors) from the womb, it was related to the concept of female hysteria in the 18th century.

CH3

1. Citoyen Touraille was the French Commander sent to St. Vincent by Victor Hugues, Governor of Guadeloupe.
2. Victor Hugues was a French revolutionary politician and colonial administrator, who governed Guadeloupe from 1794-1798.
3. On Feb 21st, 1795 a battalion of British troops was defeated by a group of rebels led by Victor Hugues in St. Lucia
4. On March 2nd, 1795 Fédon's rebellion started in Grenada.
5. "Ça ira" (French for: "It'll be fine") is an emblematic song of the French Revolution, first sung in May 1790.
6. The First Carib War was fought from 1769-1773. It ended in a stalemate marked by the signing of a peace treaty between the Black Caribs and Great Britain.
7. Based on a letter sent by Victor Hugues to the Black Caribs.
8. A reference to the Anglo-Carib Peace Treaty concluded in 1773.
9. "La Marseillaise" is a French revolutionary song which became the National Anthem of France.
10. Chief Joseph Chatoyé was the paramount chief of the Black Caribs in 1795. His name is also sometimes spelled Chatoyer in the historical record. Here Chatoyé is preferred since this is how his name was spelled in the declaration that he issued at Chateaubelair.
11. Qualibou is the Carib name for the volcanic crater (i.e., caldera) of La Soufrière volcanic crater in the neighboring island of St. Lucia. Qualibou means "at the place of death." Furthermore, there is a clear connection between Qualibou and the demon God, Qualeva. In this instance Mount Qualibou is intended to refer to the La Soufrière volcano on the island St. Vincent, which was considered by the Garifuna to be a sacred place.

CH4

1. Fédon's rebellion began in Grenada on the night of March 2nd, 1795 with attacks on the small towns of Grenville and Marquis in the East, and Gouyave in the west.

2. Governor Ninian Home was captured by rebels and held hostage at Belvidere plantation, the headquarters of Julien Fédon during the rebellion. He was eventually executed by the rebels after a failed attack on their camp by the British.

3. The 9th and 58th Regiments of Foot were based in St. George's, capital of Grenada.

4. Julien Fédon was the leader of the rebellion, along with his brother Jean-Pierre.

5. According to the historical record a specific and urgent request for gunpowder was made.

6. Kenneth Francis McKenzie was the Deputy Governor of Grenada who served as Acting Governor of the colony during Fédon's rebellion.

7. A cocoyea broom is made from the wood-like shaft of a coconut tree branch.

CH5

1. A carbet is a traditional Carib assembly house which served as the meeting and sleeping place of men.

2. At the age of four, Black Carib boys were taken from their mothers to live in the carbet with their fathers and other males.

3. According to the historical record Chief Chatoyé owned a plantation run with slave labor, near Grand Baleine, in the north of St. Vincent.

4. 'Buffalo tree' is the colloquial name in St. Vincent used to refer to a kapok or silk cotton tree.

5. The Wanaragua dance is a traditional Garifuna dance which commemorates a strategy developed by Chatoyé whereby Garifuna men disguised themselves in women's clothing in order to deceive British soldiers.

6. Tumallen is a spicy broth made from peppers, lime juice and juice extracted from the cassava plant. Ereba is flat bread made from cassava flour.

CH6

1. "The Devil's been dancing in my pocket" is an 18th century expression which means to be penniless or destitute.

2. An attorney was part of the supervisory class that managed plantations and estates. Attorneys were above overseers and bookkeepers in the social hierarchy, with responsibility for managing several estates at once and were directly answerable to the proprietor whether they were resident or absent.

3. A bookkeeper was the lowest member of the supervisory class that managed plantations and estates. Despite the name, bookkeepers had little to do with accounts. Instead, they supervised gangs of slaves who worked in sugar cane fields from dawn until midnight or in factories boiling sugar.

4. Based on historical records. Alexander Leith had close relations with several planters from Scotland including Major William Lumsden of Cushnie, Murray Farquharson of Coldrach near Ballater and Macduff Fyfe from Cabrach.

5. Alexander Leith was born into a wealthy family in Aberdeenshire, Scotland. However, due to a family disagreement his parents were left financially ruined.

6. The Ceded Isles were a group of Caribbean islands, including Dominica, Grenada, St. Vincent and Tobago, which were ceded to Great Britain in the Treaty of Paris in 1763.

7. A "maroon dinner" is a "picnic." This event is reported in the historical record.

CH7

1. An agouti is a type of rodent commonly found in St. Vincent.

2. Tafia is cheap, unaged rum made from impure molasses or sugarcane residue.

3. Yurumein means homeland in the Garifuna language. The song lyrics are original.

4. Orinagu is a reference to the Orinoco River in South America.

5. A boucan is a wooden frame or hurdle on which meat was slow-roasted and smoked. This method was also used by the Caribs to preserve the limbs of some enemies defeated in combat.

6. Karukera is the indigenous Carib name for the island of Guadeloupe.

7. This traditional Garifuna dance, still practiced to this day, is called the Chumba.

8. Vieux Fort is a town located on the southern tip of St. Lucia, which is separated from the northern tip of St. Vincent, by the St. Vincent Passage.

9. Perfidious Albion is a pejorative term used to refer to alleged acts of diplomatic sleights, duplicity, treachery and infidelity by monarchs or governments of England in their pursuit of self-interest.

CH8

1. William Greig was a prominent planter from Marriaqua, on the windward coast of St. Vincent, who warned Governor Seton of the Black Carib threat of war.
2. According to historical records, a local Carib warned William Greig to leave town since the Black Caribs planned to exterminate all the British on the island.
3. Rollo is the fictional name of the William Greig's horse in the epic poem Hiroona by Reverend Canon Horatio Nelson Huggins.

PART II: Cry of Liberty

CH9

1. The Black Caribs practiced head flattening on their newborns.
2. A reference to the Anglo-Carib Peace Treaty which was signed at the end of the First Carib War in 1773. It contains twenty-five articles and includes an oath to the King of Great Britain, George III.
3. Most Black Caribs did not speak English fluently, however, were conversant in French.
4. Garinagu is the plural form of Garifuna.

CH10

1. Fort Charlotte stands on the summit of Berkshire Hill six hundred and thirty-six feet above sea level.
2. The thirty-four canons and artillery pieces are directed inland since the British had learnt a lesson in 1779 when the French invaded the island at Calliaqua. This proved that an attack on the island could come from many possible directions, rather than directly on Kingstown or from the sea.
3. As reported in the historical record.
4. Guy Fawkes Night is an annual commemoration observed on the 5th of November to commemorate the failure of the Gunpowder Plot of 1605.
5. According to the historical record.

CH11

1. Historical records indicate that Citoyen Mather accompanied Citoyen Touraille on his mission to the Black Caribs at the behest of Governor Victor Hugues.
2. As reported in the historical record.

222

3. The name Pa Louen is a pun on the French phrase "pas loin," meaning not far away, implying that Warramou's grandfather is always close by.
4. Superstition has it that Buffalo trees, also known as silk cotton trees, house ancestral spirits and should therefore be treated with reverence.
5. Inspired by traditional aromakanis recorded by Folkways Records for the Smithsonian Museum in the 1982 album entitled Traditional Music of the Garifuna (Black Carib) Of Belize. (The folk songs recorded in this album fall in the public domain)

CH12
1. A reference to the characteristic squawking sound made by the St. Vincent Parrot (*Amazona guildingii*), which is indigenous to St. Vincent.
2. The present day location of the ruins of the estate of Madame La Croix is near the town of Mesopotamia in St. George parish in St. Vincent.

CH13
1. According to the historical record.
2. Grapeshot is a type of cannon charge consisting of small round balls, usually of lead or iron, used primarily as an antipersonnel weapon.
3. According to the historical record.
4. A poire-poudre or powder pear is a French term for a gunpowder flask.
5. "Buaidh no bàs!" means "Victory or death!" In actual fact this is the battle cry of the Scottish clans MacDougall and MacNeil.
6. According to the historical record.

CH14
1. According to the historical record.
2. According to the historical record.
3. According to the historical record.

CH15
1. "The devil take it" is a curse commonly used in the 18th century meaning "Damn it."
2. A reference to the common misconception held by European colonists that the Black Caribs practiced cannibalism. This was in fact not true.
3. When Victor Hugues disembarked in Guadeloupe on May 21st, 1794, he had a force of 1,150 soldiers. He immediately abolished slavery and in so doing rallied the slaves and 'gens de couleur' (i.e., free people of color) to join his forces to end the British occupation. By the time he

retook the island from the British on October 6th, 1794 his army had swelled to over ten thousand men, including thousands of freed slaves.

4. "My bonnie" is a period Scottish term of endearment meaning my fair or pretty one.

5. According to the historical record.

CH16

1. A reference to the Haitian revolution which had started in 1791.

2. Many French colonists supported the British occupation of Guadeloupe after Governor Hugues proclaimed the abolition of slavery on the island.

3. According to the historical record this event actually occurred.

4. Chief Chatoyé's declaration at Chateaubelair is unique since it is one of the few documents in the historical record authored by a Black Carib.

PART III: Vae Victis

CH17

1. In Amerindian cultures children were breastfed until age four or five.

2. An extended form of an ancestral Carib War cry.

CH18

1. According to the historical record.

2. A style of beard common in the late 18th century.

3. A popular hairstyle in the 18th century.

4. "As right as my leg" is an 18th century idiom equivalent to the modern day saying, "As right as rain."

5. According to the historical record, the British fort at Stubbs bay was dismantled by Duvallé's forces.

6. Frog-eaters is a derogatory period term for French people.

7. The last French occupation of the St. Vincent was from 1779-1783.

8. Admiral Jervis was the British commander who seized Martinique. He ordered the third rate ship of the line HMS *Asia* (outfitted with 64 guns), and the HMS *Zebra* to take Fort Saint Louis. Despite facing heavy fire, the *Zebra* managed to land, storm the fort and capture it. The *Zebra* lost only her pilot killed and four men wounded in the operation.

CH19

1. According to the historical record the names of the three Englishman taken prisoner by Chief Chatoyé's army at Chateaubelair were Duncan

Cruikshank, Peter Cruikshank and Alexander Grant. The name Alexander has been changed to William to avoid confusion with Alexander Leith.

2. Historical accounts report that Chatoyé personally cut each English prisoner to pieces while excoriating them at each blow.

3. Jouanacaeira is the Carib name for the island of Martinique.

CH20

1. According to the historical record.

2. According to the historical record.

3. According to the historical record.

4. Spiking a cannon and blowing its' trunnions was an effective way to render a canon inoperable. The trunnions are two projections cast just forward of the center of mass of the cannon, fixed to a two-wheeled movable gun carriage, which allow the muzzle of the canon to be raised or lowered.

CH21

1. According to the historical record.

2. As recounted in the epic poem Hiroona An Historical Romance in Poetic Form, by Reverend Canon Horatio Nelson Huggins.

3. A reference to Comet Encke which was observed in November, 1795.

CH22

1. A melee weapon is any handheld weapon used in hand-to-hand combat.

2. According to the historical record.

3. The exact circumstances of Chief Chatoyé's death are unclear in the historical record. Several different accounts of his final moments are reported with varying degrees of plausibility given the murky battlefield conditions. The most credible account suggests that he was killed by Captain Alexander Leith after receiving five bayonet thrusts in the back.

4. Captain Alexander Leith was officially credited with slaying Chief Joseph Chatoyé.

CH23

1. According to the historical record.

2. According to the historical record.

3. A reference to the valuables that Chief Chatoyé wore or had in his possession at the time of his death.

4. According to the historical record.
5. According to the historical record.
6. A dugu is a traditional extended funerary ceremony practiced by the Garifuna, lasting several nights.

CH24
1. According to the historical record Captain Alexander Leith was promoted to the rank of major in recognition of his valor in the battle for Dorsetshire Hill.
2. A reference to the Haitian Revolution and to the retaking of Guadeloupe by Governor Victor Hugues. In both cases slaves were armed with devastating consequences for French planters.

PART IV: Memento Mori

Page 180
English translation of the Carib lament from the Soufriere Foundation website. The original source of the translation is unknown.

CH25
1. According to an oral tradition that persists among residents of Chateaubelair, the site of Chief Chatoyé's final resting place lies along a ridge extending towards the center of the island, overlooking the Soufrière volcano.
2. The grave site is as described in Hiroona An Historical Romance in Poetic Form by Reverend Canon Horatio Nelson Huggins, which is consistent with known burial practices of the Kalinago.
3. A reference to an initiation test that boys aged fourteen to fifteen had to pass to become Garifuna warriors. Part of the test was to endure pain by being scratched with agouti claws and having salt rubbed into the wounds without crying out.
4. The maximum ranges of the period eight-pounder and twelve-pounder canons were 1500m (1640 yards) and 1800m (1969 yards), respectively. This means the British would not have been able to accurately fire from Fort Charlotte beyond Dorsetshire Hill and the outskirts of Kingstown.
5. Following traditional Kalinago burial practices.

CH26
1. "Jaked" is Scottish period slang term for being "drunk."

226

2. "Houghmagandie" is Scottish period slang for sexual intercourse.
3. According to the historical record.
4. According to a proclamation made by Governor Seton dated March 20th, 1795.
5. According to a communiqué from Governor Seton dated March 30th, 1795.
6. A reference to the eventual fate of the defeated Black Caribs at the end of war. According to British colonial records total of 2,248 Garifuna men women and children were deported by ship convoy to Roatan island, in present day Honduras.

CH27
1. Following traditional Kalinago burial practices.
2. Following traditional Kalinago burial practices.
3. Following Kalinago tradition when an important chief died, his favorite wife or wives were buried alive with him to escort him during his journey to the afterlife. To survive this traumatic ordeal, the wives were given a potion to drink that allowed them to sleep through the burial.

CH28
1. The maiden name of Governor Seton's wife was Susan Moray. She was the daughter of James Moray of Abercairney, in the county of Perth, Scotland. The House of Moray is also known as Clann Ruaidrí.
2. A reference to a British raid on Owia Bay that occurred later in the Second Carib War.
3. A period maritime term referring to maneuvering a ship close into shore.
4. A reference to a raid in 1794 involving the HMS *Zebra* in which Fort Saint Louis, in Martinique, was captured. This was part of an operation led by British commander, Admiral Jervis, to seize the French colony.

CH29
1. Sharpened shells from clams, mussels and other sea mollusks were implements likely used by the Kalinago to cut hair. The feasibility of doing this has been empirically demonstrated by modern historians.
2. Head shaving is a customary practice of the Kalinago during periods of mourning following the death of a family member. It offers an outward symbol of sadness and a physical reminder of loss.
3. Soli Deo Gloria (often abbreviated S.D.G.) is a Latin expression dating to the 16th century which means "Glory to God alone!"

Indigenous names for major islands in the Eastern Caribbean.

Kalinago Name	Meaning	Modern Name
Camerhogne	Land of abundance	Grenada
Hewanorra	Land of iguana*	St. Lucia
Hiroona	Land of the blessed	St. Vincent
Ichirouganaim	Red island with white teeth	Barbados
Jouanacaeira	Land of iguana*	Martinique
Karukera	Land of beautiful waters	Guadeloupe
Wai'tukubuli	Tall is her body	Dominica

*These names correspond to different species of iguana.

Bibliography

1. Huggins HN (2015). <u>Hiroona An Historical Romance in Poetic Form</u> University Press of the West Indies. (Originally published in 1930).
2. Taylor C (2012). <u>The Black Carib Wars: Freedom, Survival and the Making of the Garifuna</u>, University Press of Mississippi.
3. Moreau de Jonnès A (2002). <u>Aventures de guerre au temps de la République et du Consulat,</u> Adamant Media Corporation. (Published in French).
4. McNew N (2009). "The Second Carib War," Rocky Mountain Undergraduate Review 2.
5. Kirby IE and Martin CI (1972). "The Rise and Fall of The Black Caribs," St. Vincent and the Grenadines National Trust.
6. Sweeney JL (2007). "Caribs, Maroons, Jacobins, Brigands, and Sugar Barons: The Last Stand of the Black Caribs on St. Vincent," African Diaspora Archaeology Newsletter, Vol. 10(1): Article 7.
7. Sweeney JL (2005). "History As National Myth The War of the Brigands or the Second Carib War A Story of Vincentian Nationalism," Ph.D. Thesis, California State University.
8. Gullick CJMR (1978). "Black Carib Origins and Early Society," Proceedings of the 1977 International Congress for the Study of the Pre-Columbian Cultures of the Lesser Antilles, Université de Montreal, Montreal, pp. 283–90.
9. Hulme P (2003). "Black, Yellow, and White on St. Vincent: Moreau de Jonnès' Carib Ethnography," in Felicity A. Nussbaum, ed., The Global Eighteenth Century, pp. 182-94.
10. Kim JC (2013). "The Caribs of St. Vincent and Indigenous Resistance during the Age of Revolutions," Early American Studies, Vol. 11(1): pp. 117-32.
11. Marshall B (1973). "The Black Caribs — Native Resistance to British Penetration Into the Windward Side of St. Vincent 1763-1773," Caribbean Quarterly, Vol. 19(4), pp. 4-19.
12. González N (1983). "New evidence on the origins of the Black Carib, with thoughts on the meaning of tradition," New West Indian Guide 57 (3/4), pp. 143-72.
13. Cannon R (1851). <u>Historical archives of the Forty-sixth or South Devonshire Regiment of Foot 1779-1865</u>, Parker, Furnivall and Parker, pp. 30-33. https://archive.org/details/histrecordforty00canniala [Online, Accessed: 18th December 2022].
14. Bagneris ML (2017). <u>Colouring the Caribbean: Race and the Art of Agostino Brunias</u>, Manchester University Press.

15. Ramassote R (2020). "The Black Caribs of Central America: A problem in Three-Way of Acculturation Ruy Coelho Presentation," Vibrant: Virtual Brazilian Anthropology, Vol. 17.
https://www.redalyc.org/journal/4069/406964062031/html/
[Online, Accessed: 18th December 2022]

16. https://runaways.gla.ac.uk/minecraft/index.php/the-plantation-system-of-the-british-west-indies/
[Online, Accessed: 18th December 2022].

17. https://www.alamy.com/stock-photo/caribs.html
[Online, Accessed: 18th December 2022].

18. http://www.soufrierefoundation.org/about-soufriere/history
[Online, Accessed: 18th December 2022].

19. Duncan E (1970). A Brief History of Saint Vincent with Studies in Citizenship, Graphic Printery.

20. Anderson J (2000). Between Slavery and Freedom: Special Magistrate John Anderson's Journal of St Vincent During the Apprenticeship, University Press of the West Indies.

21. Joseph EL (2001). Warner Arundell: Adventures of a Creole, UWI Press. (Originally published in 1838).

22. Hume R (2015). "The Value of Money in Eighteenth-Century England: Incomes, Prices, Buying Power—and Some Problems in Cultural Economics," Huntington Library Quarterly, vol. 77(4), pp. 373–416.

23. The Soufrière Foundation, "History of Soufrière" [Online, Accessed: 21st October 2023].

24. Jefferson Patterson Park & Museum. "How did Native Americans cut their hair before metal tools? (OER)." https://youtu.be/U4mHStgPWWk [Online, Accessed: 20th April 2024].

230

Acknowledgments

I would like to express my sincere gratitude to the following amazing friends, family members and historians who supported me in this writing project in various invaluable ways. Noëmí Kappel, Helena Moreira Monteiro Borges, Elena Stamatelou, my father, Dr. Jeffrey Dellimore, Dr. Adrian Fraser, Prof. Curtis Jacobs, Prof. Joyce Brown, Sandra Sardinha, Angela García-Guerrero and Chrissie Thomas. Without your invaluable feedback, discerning guidance and helpful suggestions this book would not have seen the light of day.

Printed in Poland
by Amazon Fulfillment
Poland Sp. z o.o., Wrocław